3 4143 10148 8482

CAPTAIN AMERICA
THE COMING OF THE FALCON

CONTENTS

D1628310

MARVEL _POCKET BOOK_ Captain America: The Coming Of The Falcon

Captain America: The Coming Of The Falcon. Marvel Pocketbook Vol. I. Contains material originally published in magazine form as Captain America Vol. I #111-119. First printing 2014. Published by Panini Publishing, a division of Panini UK Limited. Mike Riddell, Managing Director. Alan O'Keefe, Managing Editor. Mark Irvine, Production Manager. Marco M. Lupoi, Publishing Director Europe. Samuel Taylor, Editorial Assistant. Charlotte Harvey, Designer. Office of publication: Brockbourne House, 77 Mount Ephraim, Tunbridge Wells, Kent TN4 8BS. Licensed by Marvel Characters B.V. www.marvel.com. All rights reserved. No similarity between any of the names, characters, persons and/or institutions in this edition with those of any living or dead person or institution is intended, and any such similarity which may exist is purely coincidental. This publication may not be sold, except by authorised dealers, and is sold subject to the condition that it shall not be sold or distributed with any part of its cover or markings removed, nor in a mutilated condition.

Printed in the UK.

ISBN: 978-1-84653-192-7

MIX
Paper from
responsible sources
FSC® C002386

CAPT. AMERICA
12¢ IND.
111 MAR
MARVEL COMICS GROUP
APPROVED BY THE COMICS CODE AUTHORITY
CAPTAIN AMERICA
STERANKO

[6]

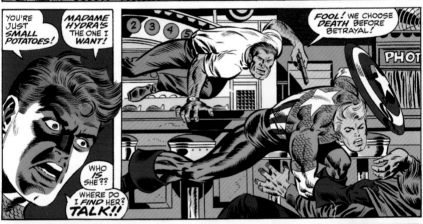

MOMENTS *LATER*...IN A HIDDEN, TORCH-LIT *CHAMBER*, WE FIND...

BRING *FORTH* THE ONE WHO *FAILED!*

HAIL HYDRA! IMMORTAL *HYDRA!*

WE SHALL *NEVER* BE DESTROYED!

CUT OFF A *LIMB*, AND TWO *MORE* SHALL TAKE ITS PLACE!

BRING *FORTH* THE ONE WHO ALLOWED THE ACCURSED *CAPTAIN AMERICA* TO ESCAPE THE TRAP OF *MADAME HYDRA!*

WE SERVE NONE BUT THE *MASTER*—

...AS THE *WORLD* SHALL SOON SERVE *US!*

BRING HIM *FORTH* THAT HE MAY LEARN HIS *FATE!*

THE FATE WHICH I DECREE TO *ALL* WHO DARE TO FOIL OUR GLORIOUS *MASTER PLAN!*

MERCY, MADAME... *MERCY!* I TRIED! I *TRIED!*

NOW HAND HIM THE HYDRA *WARRANT OF DEATH!*

NO! NO! NOT *THIS!* NOT *THIS!*

SEE HOW IT REACTS TO YOUR *OWN* BODY HEAT...

JUST AS IT WILL DO...WHEN GRASPED BY...*CAPTAIN AMERICA!*

YOU DARE SPEAK TO *ME* OF MERCY?!!

RELEASE THE ROPES! LET HIS HANDS BE *FREE!*

5

THERE'S -- **GAS** IN THE ENVELOPE! TOO LATE TO HOLD MY BREATH! I CAN **FEEL** IT... ENTERING MY NOSE...MY MOUTH... IT'S SWIRLING AROUND IN MY **BRAIN**...LIKE A WHIRL-POOL! I-I'M BEGINNING TO **SEE** THINGS...LIKE IN A STRANGE, MAD, PSYCHEDELIC **NIGHTMARE!** I'M ON A GREAT, LONELY PLAIN... RUNNING--- RUNNING--- WITH GIANT **EYES** PEERING DOWN---

...THEY'RE **MOCKING** ME...WAITING FOR ME TO REACH THE **EDGE**... OF **WHAT??** AND NOW...NOW THAT I'VE **REACHED** IT... I KNOW AT LAST... THERE'S SOMETHING--- **BEHIND** ME...!! 9

[14]

SOMETHING WENT *WRONG!* IT'S NOT *CAPTAIN AMERICA!* IT'S THE *KID!*

MADAME HYDRA WILL HAVE OUR *HEADS* FOR THIS!

DON'T *PANIC,* YOU *FOOL!* WE *STILL* HAVEN'T *FAILED!*

NOW WE *KNOW* THE SHIELD- SLINGER WILL SOON BE *AFTER* US!

HAVE TO *HURRY---* IN CASE HE COMES BACK TOO *SOON!*

TAKE HIM! HE'LL SERVE US AS A *DECOY!*

AT THAT VERY MOMENT, A WEARY *STEVE ROGERS* LEAVES HIS CAR IN THE GAR- AGE *BELOW---*

PERHAPS I'VE BEEN TOO *TOUGH,* WITH *RICK!*

YET, *ONE* MISTAKE COULD MEAN HIS *LIFE!*

I'LL HAVE ANOTHER *TALK* WITH HIM IN THE MORNING--- TRY TO *EXPLAIN* AGAIN---!

SOMEONE'S COMING!

QUICK! THE CAR'S JUST OUTSIDE!

I THOUGHT I *HEARD* SOME- THING!

MAYBE HE'S STILL *AWAKE!*

IS THAT *YOU,* SON? ARE YOU *UP?*

WAS THAT A *DOOR* SLAMMING?

WHAT'S *THIS---* ON THE *FLOOR?*

AN *ENVELOPE---* ADDRESSED TO *ME!*

RICK MUST HAVE *OPENED* IT!

BUT WHAT'S THIS STRANGE, PUNGENT *ODOR??*

AND *WHERE* IS RICK?

FOOTSTEPS--- RUNNING OUT- SIDE!

IT CAN ONLY MEAN *ONE* THING---

THEY'VE *CAPTURED RICK JONES!*

11

LIKE A MAN *POSSESSED*, THE COSTUMED *AVENGER* HURLS HIMSELF THRU THE SITTING ROOM WINDOW IN THE DIRECTION OF THE HASTY *FOOTSTEPS* HE HEARS BELOW... HEEDLESS OF THE *DANGER*... HEEDLESS OF THE *ODDS* AGAINST HIM... *ONE* ACHING THOUGHT RAGING OVER AND OVER IN HIS ANGUISHED MIND... *HIS PARTNER MUST NOT DIE AGAIN!!*

12

13.

HE'S FOUND US! STOP HIM!

BEHIND ME... A *HAMMER* BEING *COCKED!*

K!K!

WE CAN'T *STAY* HERE ANY *LONGER!* HE'S TOO *DANGEROUS!*

HURRY!! WHAT ARE YOU *WAITING* FOR?

HE'S GOT *NUMBER SEVEN!* CAN'T TAKE A CHANCE OF HIM *TALKING!*

KRAK!

OKAY... *STEP* ON IT!

THEY *SHOT* ONE OF THEIR *OWN*... JUST TO *SILENCE* HIM!

WHEN I THINK... *KILLERS,* AS BLOODTHIRSTY AS *THAT*... HAVE MADE OFF WITH *RICK*...!!

AND IT'S ALL *MY* FAULT!

I SHOULD *NEVER* HAVE GIVEN UP MY *SECRET IDENTITY!*

I'VE MADE IT TOO *EASY* FOR MY ENEMIES TO *FIND* ME... TO *ATTACK* ME!

14

I-AM-THE-*MANKILLER!*

CREATED-FOR-*ONE*-PURPOSE-ONLY--

TO-DESTROY-THE-ENEMIES-OF-HYDRA!

AN ARMORED *ROBOT*... DESIGNED AS A MAN-SHAPED *INSTRUMENT OF DEATH!*

EVEN *NOW*... AS HE BRACES TO *ATTACK*...

HIS *ARMS* HAVE SPOUTED METAL *SPIKES!*

BUT, WHATEVER *ONE* MAN CAN *DESIGN*--

ANOTHER CAN DODGE!!

BTASK!

FLANG!

AND SO, THE FIGHT RAGES ON...MAN VERSUS MACHINE...SINEWS OF FLESH AND BLOOD VERSUS CIRCUITS OF WIRE AND STEEL...WHILE, A SHORT DISTANCE AWAY, WE FIND...

THEY MENTIONED AN *AMUSEMENT ARCADE!*

I'LL START WITH THE *BIGGEST* ONE AROUND...NOT TOO *FAR* FROM HERE!

BUT... WHAT IF THERE ISN'T ENOUGH *TIME?*

WHAT IF... I'M JUST... *TOO LATE??*

THE BOY COULD *NOT* HAVE REACHED CAPTAIN AMERICA *YET*, MADAME!

NEVERTHELESS, WE TAKE NO *CHANCES!*

DRIVE *ON!*

17.

WHAT ABOUT HIS *BODY?*

IT COULDN'T JUST HAVE *VANISHED!*

THE REPORT FROM THE *LAUNCH* SAYS THE TIDES ARE RUNNING *FAST--*

HE'S PROBABLY BEEN SWEPT OUT TO *SEA* BY NOW!

THEN-- IT'S FINALLY *OVER!*

THE HORDES OF *HYDRA* HAVE *FINISHED* HIM AT LAST.

IT WAS *BOUND* TO HAPPEN-- SOONER OR LATER!! AND YET--

WHEN THE NEWS GETS *OUT--IT'S A* STORY THAT'LL *ROCK THE WORLD!!*

CAPTAIN AMERICA IS-- *DEAD!!*

A SHORT TIME LATER, AS ONE LONE COSTUMED FIGURE STANDS GUARD AT *AVENGERS HEAD-QUARTERS--*

THE SPECIAL *PHONE!*

IT MUST BE SOMETHING HIGHLY *URGENT!*

WHY DO I HAVE THIS DREAD *PREMONITION--*

THIS SENSE OF IMPENDING *TRAGEDY,??*

I HAVEN'T BEEN ABLE TO *SHAKE* THE FEELING-- SINCE *CAPTAIN AMERICA* FAILED TO MAKE HIS LAST TWO *REPORTS!*

2

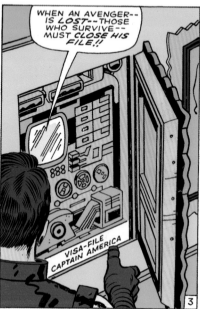

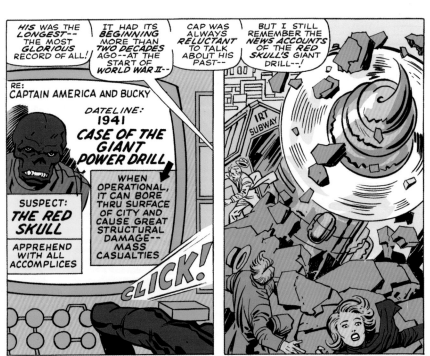

HIS was the LONGEST-- THE MOST GLORIOUS RECORD OF ALL!

IT HAD ITS BEGINNING MORE THAN TWO DECADES AGO--AT THE START OF WORLD WAR II--

CAP WAS ALWAYS RELUCTANT TO TALK ABOUT HIS PAST--

BUT I STILL REMEMBER THE NEWS ACCOUNTS OF THE RED SKULL'S GIANT DRILL--!

RE: CAPTAIN AMERICA AND BUCKY

DATELINE: 1941 CASE OF THE GIANT POWER DRILL

WHEN OPERATIONAL, IT CAN BORE THRU SURFACE OF CITY AND CAUSE GREAT STRUCTURAL DAMAGE-- MASS CASUALTIES

SUSPECT: THE RED SKULL

APPREHEND WITH ALL ACCOMPLICES

CLICK!

IRT SUBWAY

"THOUGH THE ODDS SEEMED INSURMOUNTABLE, CAP--AND HIS YOUTHFUL PARTNER, BUCKY--SAVED THE CITY FROM CERTAIN DEVASTATION--!"

4

"FINALLY, WITH HIS DEADLY HENCHMEN OUT OF ACTION, THE *RED SKULL* TRIED A DESPERATE *ESCAPE--*"

"BUT THE TWO INTREPID *SENTINELS OF LIBERTY* WERE MORE THAN EQUAL TO THE TASK--"

"AND SO THEY SCORED ONE OF THEIR *EARLIEST,* AND MOST *DRAMATIC* VICTORIES.'"

5

"ZEMO--THE HATE-OBSESSED HITLERPHILE WHO CAUSED CAPTAIN AMERICA TO FACE HIS MOST DISASTROUS DEFEAT--"

"A DEFEAT WHICH HAD ITS TRAGIC BEGINNINGS IN A SECRET ENEMY DRONE PLANE--A PLANE WHICH CAP AND BUCKY HAD BEEN ORDERED TO DESTROY--NEVER SUS- PECTING THAT IT WAS PART OF A DEMONIACAL, DEADLY TRAP--"

"AND SO--THE STAGE WAS SET--FOR MONUMENTAL TRAGEDY--!"

"IT STARTED WITH A DEAFENING ROCKET'S ROAR--AND A VALIANT, SUICIDAL CHARGE--"

8

"AND THEN IT WAS--THAT *CAPTAIN AMERICA* HEARD THE FATEFUL *SOUND*--"

"THE SOUND OF--A TICKING *BOMB!!*"

"FRANTICALLY, HE TRIED TO WARN HIS YOUTHFUL PARTNER-- BUT THE WARNING-- CAME-- *TOO LATE!!*"

"NOT EVEN THE STEEL-SINEWED FINGERS OF *STEVE ROGERS* COULD MAINTAIN HIS *GRIP* UPON THAT SLIPPERY, OIL-SPATTERED *WING*--"

"AND SO--"

"ONLY *BUCKY* WAS ABOARD--"

"WHEN THE BOOBY-TRAPPED SHIP *BLEW UP!!*"

"AS FOR THE GRIEF-STRICKEN MAN, KNOWN THRUOUT THE GLOBE AS AMERICA'S FIGHTING *SENTINEL OF LIBERTY*--"

"--THE WORLD WAS DESTINED TO HEAR OF HIM *NO MORE*--FOR TWO FATEFUL *DECADES*--AS THE SILENT CURRENT RELENTLESSLY PULLED HIM OUT TO SEA--"

"BUT, AFTER A HIATUS OF *TWENTY YEARS*--AN INSCRUTABLE *FATE* CAUSED A NEVER-TO-BE-FORGOTTEN *MEETING* TO OCCUR--"

"AS *NAMOR THE FIRST*, PRINCE OF ATLANTIS, SURFACED IN THE ICY, ARCTIC SEA--"

10

"NAMELESS *RAGE* SOON FILLED HIS *REGAL BREAST*--"

"FOR, WAS NOT HE *ALONE* THE TRUE *SUB-MARINER??*"

"AND SO, A '*NATIVE GOD*' WAS RUDELY *TOPPLED!*"

"BUT, DRIFTING SLOWLY INTO THE *WARMER,* SOUTHERN SEAS--THE ICE FINALLY *MELTED,* AND THE MOTIONLESS FIGURE FLOATED *FREE*--UNTIL--"

"THE MIGHTY *AVENGERS,* IN A PROWLING *SUBMARINE,* MADE THE MOST SENSA-TIONAL *DISCOVERY* OF THE DECADE--"

Times-Journal

CAPTAIN AMERICA RETURNS!

THAWED FROM ICE-BLOCK

NEWS-M

HE'S ALIVE

POST~RECORD

AVENGERS ON HIGH SEAS, BRING CAPTAIN AMERICA TO LIFE!

FROZEN-ALIVE FIGURE REVEALED AS VANISHED HERO OF WORLD WAR TWO

SCIENCE AMAZED! FREEZE KEPT HIM FROM AGING!

PRESS

MISSING SINCE WORLD WAR II

12

"BUT, WITHOUT HIS YOUTHFUL *PARTNER*, CAP WAS SOON TO FIND *NEW* ALLIES, SUCH AS THE *AVENGERS* THEMSELVES, AND--"

SHIELD ARMS TESTING

"*COLONEL NICK FURY*, THE HARD-BITTEN, TWO-FISTED, FIGHTING DIRECTOR OF *SHIELD*--"

"LIKE SO *MANY* WORLD-FAMED ADVENTURERS, THEIR LIVES AND EXPLOITS WERE DESTINED TO BECOME DRAMATICALLY *INTER-MINGLED*--"

"WHILE THE MOST *POWERFUL* ELEMENT *LINKING* CAPTAIN AMERICA TO SHIELD SOON PROVED TO BE--"

"--A COURAGEOUS, CAPTIVATING *FEMALE* NAMED *SHARON CARTER*--BETTER KNOWN TO FURY'S FILES AS-- *AGENT THIRTEEN!*"

SHIELD AGENT 13

"*SHARON CARTER*-- THE GIRL WHO WON STEVE'S *HEART!*"

14

"HOW MANY *TIMES* HAD THE RED-WHITE-AND-BLUE *AVENGER* COURTED DEATH ITSELF TO FIGHT SIDE-BY-SIDE WITH THE GIRL HE *LOVED?*"

"--SUCH AS THE TIME HE DARED FACE THE WRATH OF *MODOK* HIMSELF.'"

"*MODOK*--MONSTROUS RULER OF THE SECRET ARMY KNOWN AS *A.I.M.!*"

"*MODOK*--WHO HAD NEVER BEFORE BEEN *DEFIED*--LET ALONE *DEFEATED.'*"

"*MODOK*--WHOSE HIGHLY-TRAINED, MURDEROUS *AGENTS* WERE AMONG THE MOST *FEARED* FIGHTING MEN ON EARTH!'"

"BUT, FEAR WAS A *STRANGER* TO THE MAN CALLED *CAPTAIN AMERICA*--"

"AND SO, TODAY, *MODOK* AND HIS MURDERERS MENACE THE WORLD *NO MORE.'*"

15

"IT FINALLY SEEMED AS THOUGH THE *HAPPINESS*, WHICH HAD BEEN SO LONG *DENIED* TO STEVE ROGERS, MIGHT BE HIS *AT LAST!*"

"TOGETHER WITH THE GIRL HE LOVED, HE MIRACULOUSLY LEAPT FROM *TRIUMPH* TO *TRIUMPH*--"

"UNTIL IT SEEMED THAT *NO FOE* COULD BEAT HIM-- *NO DANGER* COULD *STOP* HIM!"

"--NOT EVEN WHEN THE VERY *EARTH* EXPLODED BENEATH THEIR FEET--"

"--AND ONE OF THE MOST MANIACALLY *MACABRE* MENACES OF ALL ERUPTED INTO VIEW--"

"IT WAS *THEN*--AS A SHOCKED HUMAN RACE WILL NEVER *FORGET*--THAT THE *RED SKULL'S* MOST CATACLYSMIC CREATION THREATENED TO *DESTROY ALL OF MANKIND!!*"

"AND THERE WAS NONE BUT *CAPTAIN AMERICA* TO OPPOSE HIM!"

16

"NONE BUT THE INDOMITABLE *SENTINEL OF LIBERTY*--AND A FRAIL THOUGH VALIANT *FEMALE* WHO WOULD NEVER LEAVE HIS SIDE--TO FACE THE BLUDGEONING, ALMOST INCONCEIVABLE *POWER* OF--"

"--THE FANTASTIC *FOURTH SLEEPER!*"

17

"BUT, THE COURAGE, THE DEDICATION, THE INCREDIBLE *SKILL* OF THE SHIELD-SLINGING SENTINEL *SMASHED* THE FINAL SLEEPER-- AND A HOST OF *OTHER* COLORFUL FOES AS WELL--FOES SUCH AS *BATROC, THE LEAPER*--"

"AND THE TANTALIZING *TUMBLER*--"

"NOT TO MENTION THE ALWAYS DANGEROUS *SWORDSMAN*--"

"--OR, SUCH SUPER-POWERED MENACES AS THE *LIVING LASER!*"

18

"WHERE *OTHER* MEN MIGHT *FALTER*--SUCH AS THE TIME STEVE SEEMED *TRAPPED* BY THE RED SKULL'S BAND OF MERCILESS *EXILES*--"

"*CAPTAIN AMERICA* MERELY FOUGHT ALL THE *HARDER*-- KNOWING THAT *LIBERTY* ITSELF WAS EVER AT STAKE!"

19

"AND, AS THE TERRIFYING *TRAPSTER* WAS SOON TO FIND OUT--*NEVER* DID A MAN USE ONE SINGLE *WEAPON*--"

"--THE WAY *CAP* USED HIS SYMBOLIC, STREAKING *SHIELD!*"

S*NAP!*

"BUT, EVEN WHEN BATTLING THE BLUDGEONING FORCE OF A *DR. FAUSTUS*--"

"--HIS *GREATEST* WEAPON-- HIS MOST *INFALLIBLE* WEAPON-- WAS, AS ALWAYS--"

"--THE FURY OF-- HIS FLAILING *FISTS!*"

AND NOW-- IT'S *ENDED!*

OUR MOST HONORED *FREEDOM FIGHTER,* STRUCK DOWN IN HIS *PRIME*--

--BY THE HATE-FILLED HORDES OF *HYDRA!*

PAP FILL

REST EASY, SOLDIER--

YOU WILL BE *AVENGED!*

NEXT: THINGS ARE *NEVER* WHAT THEY *SEEM!*

20

CAPT.
AMERICA
12¢ 113
IND MAY

MARVEL
COMICS
GROUP

CAPTAIN AMERICA

IN
MEMORIAM

CAPTAIN
AMERICA
DIED
1968
IN THE
SERVICE
OF HIS
COUNTRY

STERANKO

[49]

"FOR YEARS, I STRUGGLED FOR MERE *SURVIVAL*-- LIVING BY MY *WITS* AS BEST I COULD! WITH NONE TO *GUIDE* ME-- WITH NONE TO *CARE!* I DRIFTED INTO A LIFE OF *CRIME*--CULMINATING WITH THE DEATH OF *BARON STRUCKER*--WHEN, AT THE TOUCH OF A *BUTTON*--"

--I *ELIMINATED* THOSE OF *HIGHEST* HYDRA RANK--

SO THAT *I*, IN THIS *SECTOR* WOULD THEN BECOME-- *SUPREME HYDRA!*

BUT, *NEVER* CAN I ESCAPE THE TYRANNY OF--*MY MIRROR!*

I KEEP *READING* THE WORDS-- OVER AND *OVER* AGAIN--

BUT, THEY *DON'T REGISTER!* THEY DON'T REALLY *SINK IN!*

I CAN'T MAKE MYSELF *BELIEVE* THEM.'.' I *CANT--*.'.'

HAVE TO SNAP *OUT* OF IT! CAN'T GO *ON* LIKE THIS!

IN THE NEXT ROOM --THE *AVENGERS* ARE ASSEMBLED!

I MUSTN'T--KEEP THEM *WAITING!*

THE *YOUTH* APPROACHES!

WE KNOW HOW *DIFFICULT* THIS IS FOR YOU, SON!

IT ISN'T EASY-- FOR *ANY* OF US!

BUT, WE HAVE TO LEARN EXACTLY WHAT *HAPPENED!*

THUS, WE BID THEE--*SPEAK!*

A SHORT TIME LATER, WITHIN THE AUSTERE CONFINES OF A MIDTOWN FUNERAL PARLOR--

WILL YOU ALL PLEASE COME THIS WAY?

AMONG THE MOURNERS ARE THE MEN HE HAD FOUGHT BESIDE--AND THE GIRL WHO HAD WON HIS HEART--

IF ONLY--IT WERE A DREAM!

IF ONLY IT WEREN'T SO BRUTALLY --SO TERRIBLY REAL!

THE CASKET IN FRONT OF YOU CONTAINS A DUMMY--

'CAUSE WE NEVER FOUND STEVE'S BODY!

BUT WE WEREN'T ABOUT TO LET THAT STOP US-- FROM GIVIN' CAP THIS TRIBUTE!

ANYTHING WE SAY IS JUST TO MAKE US FEEL BETTER--

'CAUSE CAPTAIN AMERICA DOESN'T NEED OUR PRAISE!

HIS WHOLE LIFE--AND THE WAY HE LIVED IT--WAS THE GREATEST EPITAPH A GUY COULD HAVE!

7

THE *GAS* WAS AS FAST-ACTING --AS *EFFECTIVE* --AS *MADAME HYDRA* PROMISED!

AND THEY NEVER *SUSPECTED* A THING!

QUICKLY NOW! BACK INTO OUR *HYDRA* GARB!

PHASE ONE HAS PRO-CEEDED *PERFECTLY,* MADAME!

NOW PREPARE FOR-- *PHASE TWO!*

HAIL HYDRA! IMMORTAL *HYDRA!* WE SHALL *NEVER* BE DESTROYED!

CUT OFF A LIMB-- AND TWO *MORE* SHALL TAKE ITS PLACE!

NOT ONLY HAVE WE DESTROYED *CAPTAIN AMERICA--*

BUT THE *AVENGERS* AS WELL!

MEANWHILE, OUTSIDE--

THAT'S FUNNY! EVERYTHING'S *LOCKED UP!*

BUT--IT DOESN'T MAKE *SENSE!*

THE AVENGERS *SAID* THEY'D BE HERE MOST OF THE *NIGHT--* TILL THE *FUNERAL* TOMORROW!

HEY! WHAT'S *THAT?*

HYDRA! LOADING THOSE *BINS* INTO WAITING CARS!

10

I DUNNO WHAT IT *MEANS*-- BUT I KNOW I'VE GOTTA *FOLLOW* THEM!

*S*LOWLY, SILENTLY, THE GRIM, MOTORIZED CARAVAN MAKES ITS WAY THRU THE FOG-SHROUDED STREETS, UNTIL--

TAXI STAND

KEEP *GOING!* THE GATES ARE *OPEN!*

THEY'VE *STOPPED!* THIS IS MY CHANCE TO TAKE *COVER!*

BUT-- WHAT IF-- THE *AVENGERS* ARE IN THOSE *BINS??*

DREARCLIFF CEMETERY

CAN'T AFFORD TO *WAIT* ANY LONGER!

YOU'LL WAIT! UNLESS YOU WANT TO *GET* IT--RIGHT *NOW!*

11

SUDDENLY, THE SCENE IS SHATTERED BY A NERVE-SEARING ROAR OF DEFIANCE, AS A DOZEN HYDRA KILLERS WHIRL ABOUT TO SEE A HIGH-POWERED MOTORCYCLE LEAPING FROM THE CREST OF A HILL! AND, AS THE THUNDERING MACHINE SPLAYS THE MARBLE AND GRANITE OF BATTERED TOMB-STONES IN ITS PATH, A SINEWY RED, WHITE AND BLUE THUNDERBOLT, ON A MISSION OF VENGEANCE, SMASHES INTO THEIR MIDST...

CAPTAIN AMERICA LIVES!

A *MAN* CAN BE DESTROYED! A *TEAM*, OR AN *ARMY* CAN BE DESTROYED! BUT, HOW DO YOU DESTROY AN *IDEAL*--A *DREAM*? HOW DO YOU DESTROY A LIVING *SYMBOL*--OR HIS INDOMITABLE *WILL*--HIS UNQUENCHABLE *SPIRIT*? PERHAPS *THESE* ARE THE THOUGHTS WHICH THUNDER WITHIN THE MURDEROUS *MINDS* OF THOSE WHO HAVE CHOSEN THE WAY OF *HYDRA*--OF THOSE WHO FACE THE *FIGHTING FURY* OF FREEDOM'S MOST FEAR- LESS *CHAMPION*--THE GALLANT, RED-WHITE-AND-BLUE-GARBED FIGURE WHO HAS BEEN A TOWERING SOURCE OF *INSPIRATION* TO LIBERTY-LOVERS EVERYWHERE! HOW CAN THE FEARSOME FORCES OF *EVIL* EVER HOPE TO DESTROY THE UNCONQUER- ABLE *CAPTAIN AMERICA?*

RICK! GRAB A PISTOL!

I'LL HOLD THEM OFF WHILE YOU DO IT, BOY!

EVERYTHING DEPENDS ON THE NEXT FEW SECONDS!!

THERE! ON THE GROUND! GET IT!!

HE'S GOT SOMETHING IN MIND!

--AND I'M NOT GONNA FAIL HIM!

NO MATTER WHAT--I WON'T LET HIM DOWN!

NOW STAND THERE--WITH IT POINTED THIS WAY!

NO MATTER WHAT HAPPENS --HOLD YOUR GROUND!!

I'M COMING TOWARDS YOU NOW!

THEY SHOULD BE BEHIND ME --ALL BUNCHED TOGETHER--JUST AS I PLANNED!

NOW--AIM AT THE GAS TANK OF MY FALLEN CYCLE!

IT'S FILLED WITH A SPECIAL EXPLOSIVE FUEL!!

AS SOON AS THEY'RE NEAR IT-- FIRE!!

GOTCHA, CAP!

16

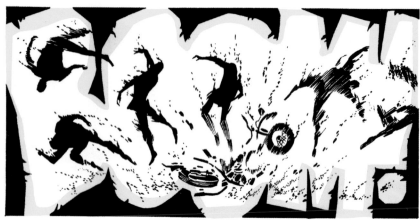

NOW THERE'S NO ONE *LEFT*-- BUT *MADAME HYDRA!*

BUT SHE CAN *KEEP!* WE'VE GOT TO CHECK ON THE *AVENGERS!*

LUCKILY, THEY'RE *ALL RIGHT!*

I SUSPECT THEY'RE FAR LESS *HELPLESS* THAN HYDRA *THOUGHT!*

CAP!! *BEHIND* YOU--RIGHT NEAR THAT *CRYPT!*

WATCH IT! SHE'S *UP* TO SOME-THING!

I'VE *FAILED!* I'VE LOST *EVERY-THING!*

AND NOW-- ACCORDING TO THE *CODE OF HYDRA*--

MY OWN *LIFE* MUST BE *FORFEIT!*

IT IS ONLY *FITTING* --IT IS ONLY *RIGHT!*

BUT, I CAN *STILL* MAKE AMENDS--STILL *SAVE MYSELF*--

BY *DESTROYING* OUR GREATEST *ENEMIES!*

HUNTER MISSILES!! COMING RIGHT *AT* US!

17

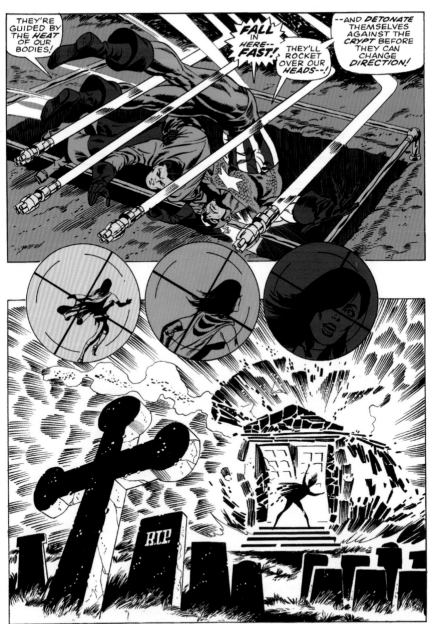

CALL IT *DESTINY*--OR THE WONDROUS WORKINGS OF *FATE*--OR MERELY ANOTHER OF LIFE'S INEXPLICABLE *IRONIES*...CALL IT WHAT YOU WILL--BUT, IN A MATTER OF *SPLIT-SECONDS*, SHE WHO HAD BEEN *MADAME HYDRA* REAPS THE GRIM HARVEST SHE HAD SO MERCILESSLY *SOWN*--!

THE BATTLE IS *NEVER* ENDED, RICK!

THERE WILL BE *OTHERS* TO TAKE HER PLACE!

THAT'S THE REASON I INFLATED A *RUBBERIZED FIGURE*, DRESSED IN MY *OWN* HELMET AND SHIRT!

IT WAS THAT *FIGURE*--WEARING A STEVE ROGERS *FACE MASK*--WHICH YOU SAW *FIRED* UPON--AND *HIT!*

AND *NOW*, THOUGH THE WORLD WILL REALIZE THAT *CAPTAIN AMERICA* STILL LIVES--

NONE CAN BE SURE *WHO* IS THE MAN BENEATH THE MASK!

--AND SO, CAPTAIN AMERICA HAS A *SECRET IDENTITY* ONCE MORE!

CEMETERY

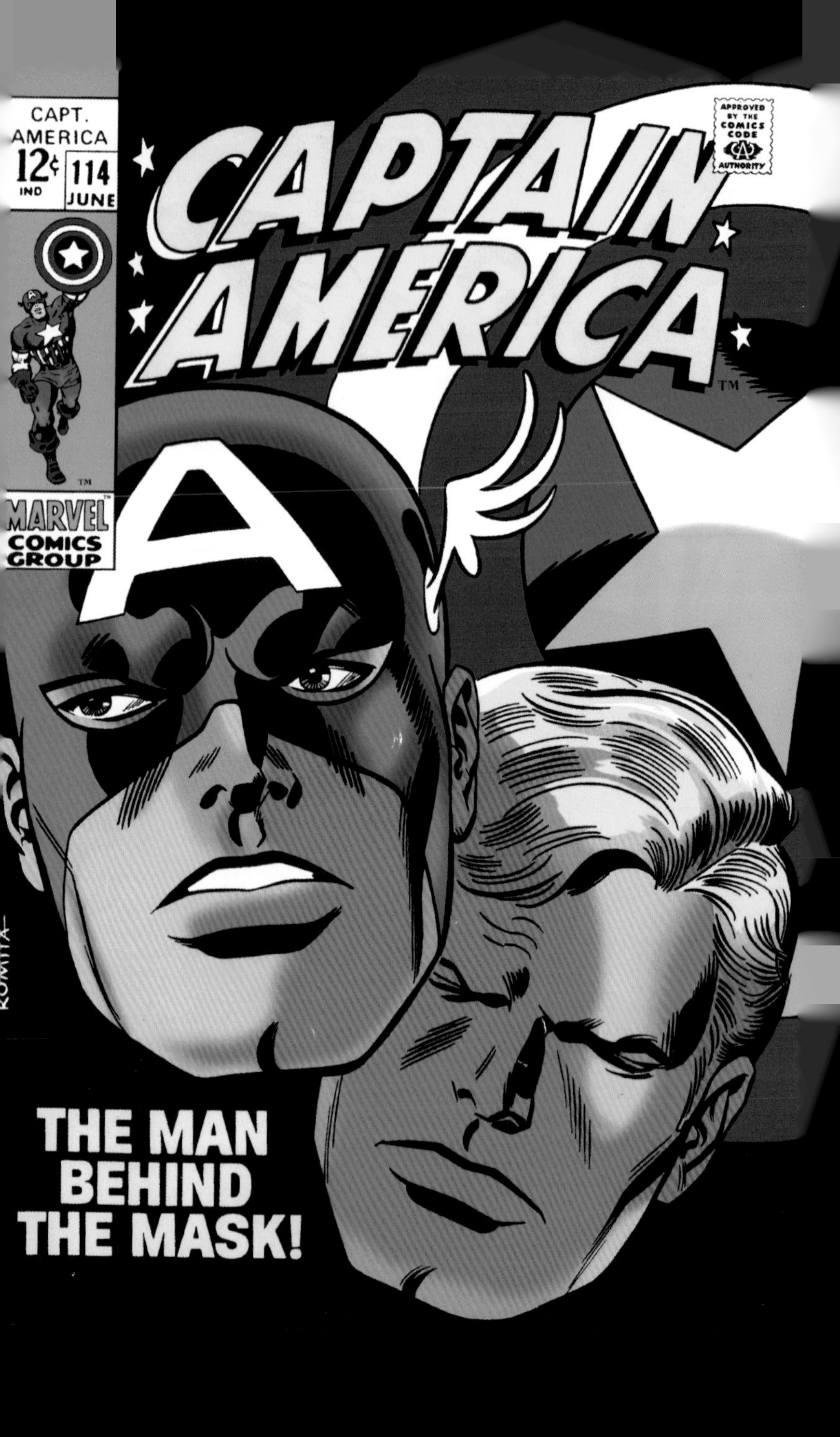
CAPT. AMERICA
12¢
IND
114
JUNE
APPROVED BY THE COMICS CODE AUTHORITY
CAPTAIN AMERICA
TM
MARVEL COMICS GROUP
KOMITA
THE MAN BEHIND THE MASK!

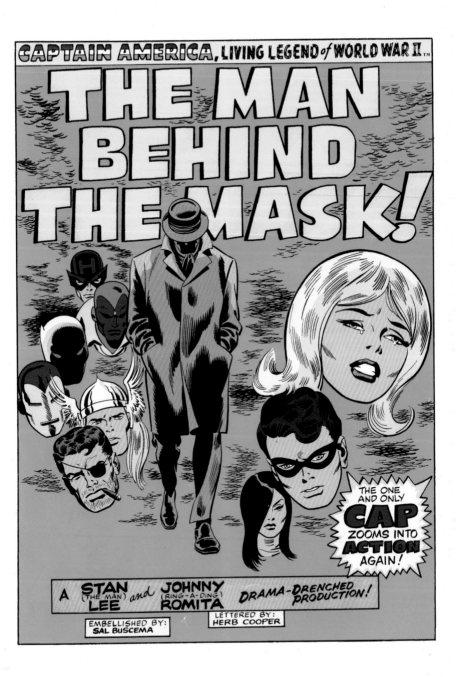

I'VE *DONE* IT --AT LAST! I'VE *FINALLY* CONVINCED THE WORLD THAT *STEVE ROGERS* IS *DEAD!*

THAT MEANS *CAPTAIN AMERICA* WILL HAVE A *SECRET IDENTITY* ONCE MORE!

AND THOSE WHOSE *LIVES* ARE CLOSEST TO MINE--

SHARON-- AND *RICK*-- WILL BE IN *LESS DANGER*--

BECAUSE IF MY *ENEMIES* DON'T KNOW WHERE-- OR WHO-- I REALLY *AM*--

THEY'LL HAVE A *TOUGHER* TIME FINDING *THEM!*

SO, IT'S *FAREWELL* TO THE MAN KNOWN AS *STEVE ROGERS!*

AND YET-- HOW CAN YOU SAY *FAREWELL* --TO A MAN WHO NEVER *LIVED?*

CAN I TRUTHFULLY SAY STEVE ROGERS WAS *EVER* MORE THAN JUST A *NAME?*

DID HE EVER REALLY HAVE A *LIFE*--A MEANINGFUL *IDENTITY*-- TO CALL HIS *OWN?*

NO! EVER SINCE *ADULTHOOD*-- I'VE LIVED UNDER THE ALL-PERVASIVE SHADOW OF *CAPTAIN AMERICA!*

MY *COSTUME* HAS BECOME AS MUCH A *PART* OF ME--AS MY *SKIN!*

IT'S ONLY WHEN I DRESS IN *CIVVIES*--AS I'M DOING *NOW*--THAT I FEEL LIKE A *PRETENDER!*

EVEN MY *LODGING*--THE VERY *ROOF* OVER MY HEAD--IS IN *AVENGERS HEADQUARTERS!*

I'VE NEVER HAD A *HOME*--THAT I COULD CALL MY *OWN!*

AND *NOW*--UNCONSCIOUSLY--AUTOMATICALLY--I'M HEADING THERE *AGAIN!*

BUT, I *MUSTN'T!* I HAVE TO *BREAK* WITH THE PAST --ONCE AND FOR *ALL!*

SOMEHOW *WAY*--I'VE GOT TO START A *LIFE* FOR MYSELF!

NOW THAT WE KNOW HE IS STILL *ALIVE*--WHY HASN'T *CAPTAIN AMERICA* BEEN HEARD FROM?

FUNNY--FOR A MINUTE I THOUGHT *THAT* WAS HIM--DOWN THERE!

BUT OL' WINGHEAD WOULDN'T HAVE *TURNED*--AND WALKED *AWAY* LIKE THAT!

THE *PANTHER* CANNOT BE *FOOLED* BY ANOTHER'S *GAIT!*

MANY TIMES HAVE I OBSERVED THE *MOVEMENTS* OF THE RED-WHITE-AND-BLUE SENTINEL--AND NOW I SAY TO YOU--

THE FIGURE *BELOW*, FADING AMIDST THE SHADOWS OF NIGHT, IS TRULY --*CAPTAIN AMERICA!*

THEN HE DOES NOT *WISH* TO JOIN US!

3

WHATEVER THAT GENT DOES--HE'S GOT HIS REASONS!

STILL, IT IS STRANGE THAT HE WOULDN'T CHECK BACK HERE-- ESPECIALLY AFTER HIS VICTORY OVER MADAME HYDRA!

TO A MAN WITH A LIFETIME OF VICTORIES BEHIND HIM--

ANOTHER ONE CAN MAKE LITTLE DIFFERENCE!

REMEMBER, LADY-- EVEN MADAME HYDRA WASN'T THE SUPREME LEADER!

SHE JUST LED THE HYDRA GOONS IN THE NEW YORK AREA!

WILL WE EVER FIND THE ONE WHO IS THE SECRET MASTER-- OF ALL THE EVIL HORDE?

IF IT CAN BE DONE-- SOMEWHERE IN THE DARKNESS--OUT THERE-- IS THE ONE MAN WHO WILL SOME DAY DO IT!

AND, WHATEVER HIS REASONS MAY BE FOR SEEKING PRIVACY, AND SOLITUDE--

WE MUST RESPECT HIS WISHES--UNTIL WE MEET AGAIN!

MOMENTS LATER--

I CAN'T WAIT ANY LONGER!

I HAVE TO SEE SHARON--HEAR HER VOICE-- TOUCH HER LIPS!

BARBER

NICK FURY WILL KNOW WHERE TO FIND HER!

BUT, I DARE NOT GO IN LIKE THIS--WITH- OUT MY MASK!

NOT EVEN THE AGENTS OF SHIELD MUST EVER AGAIN SEE ME AS STEVE ROGERS!

THE FEWER THAT KNOW MY SECRET--

THE SAFER IT WILL BE!

4

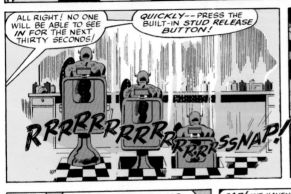

AT THAT MOMENT, WITHIN THE *DEAD CENTER* OF TARGET AREA M, WE FIND--

I'VE ALREADY *CUT* THE ALARM-- *NEUTRALIZING* IT!

WHICH MEANS--THERE'S A CHANCE FOR ME TO *REACH* THEM-- TO TAKE THEM BY *SURPRISE!*

AND--IF I *FAIL*--AT LEAST I'LL KNOW I *TRIED!*

JUST AS *STEVE* TRIED--BEFORE HE WAS-- *CUT DOWN!*

THE ONLY MAN I EVER LOVED-- GAVE HIS *LIFE*-- FOR THOSE HE LEFT BEHIND!

NOW--HOW CAN *I* DO-- ANY *LESS?!!*

THA-K!

STAY WHERE YOU *ARE!!* YOU'RE ALL *UNDER ARREST!* YOU'RE PRISONERS OF SHIELD!!

ONE LONE *FEMALE!* HOW IS IT *POSSIBLE?*

THERE MUST BE A *BRIGADE* BEHIND HER!

NO! *WAIT!* IT'S A TRICK! SHE'S ALONE!

THERE'S *NOBODY* WITH HER!

USE YOUR *WEAPONS!*

SHE MUST NOT *ESCAPE!*

7

BUT THEN--

BTANNGG!

IT-IT CAN'T BE--!!

BUT IT IS! IT IS!!

HEADS UP, DARLING!!

IT'S A BRAND-NEW BALL GAME NOW!

CAP!! YOU'RE ALIVE!! I DON'T KNOW HOW-- BUT IT'S TRUE-- YOU'RE ALIVE!!

THEY *BUILT* HIM TO BE *IMPERVIOUS* TO WEAPONS!!

NOW GET *BACK*--TAKE A *BREATHER!*

DO EXACTLY AS I *SAY!*

HE'S JUST A *MACHINE*--DOING WHAT HE WAS *BUILT* TO DO!

BUT *ANY* MACHINE CAN HAVE--A FATAL *FLAW!*

RICK! TRY OPERATION *UPSET!!* ONE--TWO--

THREE!

WE MANAGED TO *TOPPLE* HIM!

PERFECT! BY STRIKING JUST THE RIGHT *PRESSURE POINTS*--

IT'S LIKE--A LIVING NIGHT-MARE!

LIKE BEING TRAPPED ON A TREADMILL--WITH NO WAY TO GET OFF!

I COULDN'T LOSE SOMEONE CLOSE TO ME--A SECOND TIME!

AND YET--SHARON--AND RICK--HOW LONG CAN THEIR LUCK HOLD OUT??

MINUTES LATER, IN A RESTAURANT WASHROOM, AFTER CAUTIOUSLY BUYING SOME SPECIAL ITEMS--

AS SOON AS I'M ALONE HERE--I'LL MAKE CERTAIN THAT MY TRUE IDENTITY REMAINS A SECRET!

AND THEN, I'LL FIND A ROOM FOR MYSELF!

HOTELS...

BUT I CAN'T SIGN A REGISTER--AS STEVE ROGERS!

I DARE NOT DO ANYTHING --AS STEVE ROGERS!

SO FAR AS THE WORLD KNOWS--STEVE ROGERS IS DEAD!

AND THAT'S THE WAY--IT'S GOT TO BE!

BUT THEN...

NO LUGGAGE? I'M SORRY, SIR!

YOU SAY YOU HAVE NO IDENTIFICATION?

WE'RE ALL FILLED UP!

WHAT? NO HOME ADDRESS?

THIS IS VERY IRREGULAR!

I'M SORRY, SIR!

NO DRIVER'S LICENSE? NO CREDIT CARDS? AND YOU'RE NOT EVEN SURE OF YOUR NAME!

TRY SOMEPLACE ELSE, MISTER!

I CAN'T EVEN THINK OF THE RIGHT ANSWERS TO GIVE!

MY BRAIN JUST KEEPS REPEATING --SHARON! SHARON!

18

BUT FINALLY, IN A SEEDY, SIDE-STREET *HOTEL*, IN A SHODDY, RUN-DOWN NEIGHBORHOOD--

THAT'LL BE *TEN BUCKS* FOR THE WEEK-- IN *ADVANCE!*

AND WE DON'T RENT TO *TROUBLE-MAKERS!*

IT'S MY *LAST* TEN DOLLARS--

BUT I CAN'T JUST WALK THE *STREETS* ALL NIGHT!

CAPTAIN AMERICA-- THE FAMOUS *SENTINEL* OF LIBERTY--

--THE *LIVING LEGEND* OF WORLD WAR TWO!!

WITHOUT MY *COSTUME* I'M A *NO-BODY*--A *NOTHING*--

LUCKY TO GET A *ROOM*-- IN A *NOWHERE* HOTEL!

IS *THIS* THE WAY IT MUST BE-- FOR THE REST OF MY *LIFE?*

MUST I LIVE OUT THE *REST* OF MY DAYS AS A HUMAN *SYMBOL*--

AS AN *EMOTIONLESS*, *MASKED* *FIGHTING MACHINE??*

IT *CAN'T* BE THE SUM TOTAL OF MY ENTIRE-- *WHA*--??!

A SUDDEN, SILENT *SHOCK*-- LIKE SOME STRANGE *SHIFTING* OF *TIME AND SPACE* ITSELF !!

A *FORM*-- MATERIALIZING IN THE DARK-- *NO!*

IT *CAN'T* --IT *CAN'T BE!!*

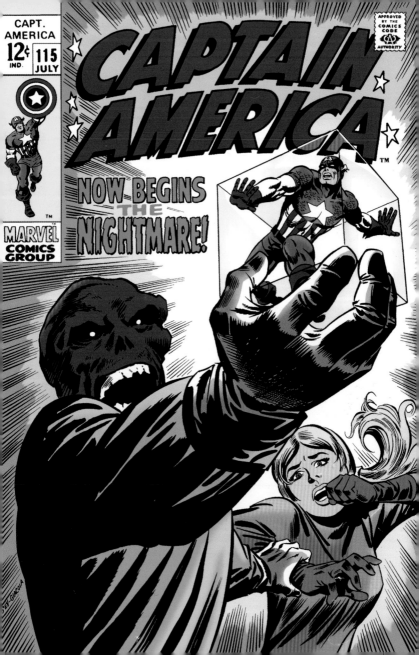

BE *SILENT,* DOOMED ONE! *REMEMBER* ...YOU WILL *LIVE* ONLY AS LONG AS *I* PERMIT IT!

AND, IF YOU THINK YOU CAN WREST THIS WEAPON *FROM ME...* YOU ARE *WRONG...!* FOR IT IS NO MERE *PISTOL* THAT I HOLD...

...BUT THE *COSMIC CUBE* ITSELF!!

THE INVINCIBLE, OMNIPOWERFUL *CUBE...* WHICH CAN ASSUME *ANY FORM* I WILL IT TO!

IT WA --BUT PAY

I HOPI OFF-L WOUL HIM O ACTI

YES...THE MOST *WONDROUS* OF ALL OBJECTS IS *MINE* ONCE MORE!

AND SO... THE *RED SKULL* ALONE ...CONTROLS THE FATE OF THE *WORLD!*

BUT, I WANT TO *SAVOR* MY *TRIUMPH!* I WANT TO SEE YOU *CRINGE* BEFORE ME... AS *CAPTAIN AMERICA!*

AND, SO LONG AS I HOLD THE *COSMIC CUBE...*

WHATEVER THE *SKULL DESIRES* ...MUST INSTANTLY *COME TO PASS!*

SHE'S OF THE NOW'. CHAN

2.

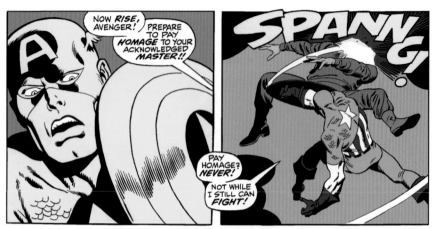

LIBERTY-LOVING *FOOL.!!* I WAS NEVER THERE IN THE *FIRST* PLACE!

DID YOU *THINK* I'D ALLOW *YOU* TO ATTACK THE MIGHTY *HOLDER* OF THE *COSMIC CUBE!*

I MERELY ALLOWED YOU THE *ILLUSION* OF COMBAT...TO MAKE YOUR CRAVEN *DOWN-FALL* ALL THE MORE *IGNOBLE!*

THUMMP!!

NOW *LIE* THERE, YOU SWINE...AS I *REVEL* IN YOUR LASTING *DEFEAT!*

OF ALL WHO *LIVE*... NONE HAVE BEEN *BETTER* SCHOOLED IN *VILLAINY* THAN THE *RED SKULL!*

TIME AND *AGAIN,* I HAD ALMOST ATTAINED MY ETERNAL *GOAL*... THE DOWNFALL OF *AMERICA* --- THE CRUSHING OF *LIBERTY* THRUOUT THE GLOBE...

...ONLY TO HAVE *YOU* SNATCH MY VICTORIES *FROM* ME!

BUT SOON... YOU WILL TROUBLE ME *NO LONGER!*

4

HOW DID YOU **DO** IT?? HOW DID YOU... **REGAIN** THE CUBE?

I THOUGHT...IT WAS **LOST**... FOREVER!

HAH! YOU WOULD **LIKE** TO KNOW THAT...**WOULDN'T** YOU?

OR, DO YOU MERELY WANT TO KEEP ME **TALKING**...WHILE YOU DESPERATELY PLAN AN **ESCAPE?**

AS THOUGH ESCAPE CAN BE **POSSIBLE**... FROM THE HOLDER OF THE **COSMIC CUBE!!**

BUT, THE LONGER I LET YOU **LIVE**... IN ABJECT **HELPLESSNESS** ...THE GREATER MY **TRIUMPH** SHALL BE!

AND SO, YOU SHALL **HAVE** YOUR ANSWER!

...WHILE YOU **TREMBLE** BEFORE ME...WONDERING WHEN...AND **HOW**...I SHALL ELECT TO **CRUSH** YOU!

SINCE YOU CAUSED ME TO **LOSE** THE FATEFUL CUBE... MONTHS AGO, BENEATH THE SEA*... I HAVE NEVER STOPPED **SEARCHING**...**SEEKING**.. PROBING!

LED BY MY LOYAL BAND OF **EXILES**, SHARP-EYED **AGENTS** THRU'OUT THE WORLD KEPT **WATCH** FOR ME!

AND THEN, AT **LAST**, MY VIGIL WAS RE-WARDED..!

*AND WHERE WERE **YOU** WHEN IT HAPPENED IN ISH #81?
-- SNOOPY STAN.

"IT BEGAN WITH THE **ERUPTION** OF A SMOLDERING **VOLCANO**, JUST OFF THE **MEDITERRANEAN**---"

"A FIERY VOLCANO WHICH SPEWED FORTH TONS OF MOLTEN **LAVA**...**FLAME** ...AND BILLOWING **SMOKE**...AND ONE THING **MORE**..."

"---A SMALL, GLEAM-ING **CUBE**... WHICH RESTED ON THE SHORE, GLOWING WITH AN EERIE, MYSTIC **LIGHT**, UNTIL..."

A STRANGELY SHINING **OBJECT!** WHAT CAN IT **BE?**

"THE UNSUSPECTING OAF CALMLY **POCKETED** THE MOST POWERFUL OBJECT ON EARTH ---AND THEN..."

"BRINGING IT TO HIS LONELY SHACK, HE UNTHINKINGLY MADE A **WISH**..."

IF ONLY **WE** COULD DINE AS THEY DO IN THE **PALACE**! I WISH--- **MADRE DIOS!!**

IT IS A **MIRACLE!**

6

[95]

"EVEN A WITLESS *PEASANT* SUCH AS *HE* SOON REALIZED WHAT HE HAD *FOUND!*"

"BUT, THE HUMBLE FOOL TRIED TO USE IT FOR *GOOD*...TO MAKE HIS LITTLE *ISLAND* A BETTER PLACE TO *LIVE!*"

"*AND THAT* WAS HIS *UN-DOING...!*"

"MY BAND OF *EXILES* SOON LEARNED OF THE SUDDEN *PROSPERITY* OF ONE LONE VILLAGE... AND THEY BROUGHT ME THE *NEWS!*"

OF *COURSE!* IT *HAS* TO BE THE *CUBE!* THERE CAN BE *NO OTHER* EXPLANATION!

AFTER ALL THESE *MONTHS*...ALL THIS *WAITING*...I'VE *FOUND* IT AT LAST!

DO NOT *FORGET*... IT WAS *WE* WHO BROUGHT YOU THE *NEWS!*

YOU SHALL *HAVE* YOUR REWARDS... ONCE THE CUBE IS *MINE!*

BUT *NOW*... NOTHING MUST *STOP* US!

THE PLANE IS *READY*, MASTER!

THEN WE LEAVE *AT ONCE!*

"THE *REST* WAS ROUTINE! WITHIN A MATTER OF *MINUTES* WE HAD REACHED OUR DESTINATION..."

"*AND THEN*...AS FATE HAD SURELY *IN-TENDED*...THE CUBE AGAIN WAS *MINE!*"

7.

"IT WAS THE GREATEST MOMENT OF MY *LIFE*... THE CULMINATION OF ALL MY *DREAMS!* I STOOD *FINGERING* IT... *STUDYING* IT... *TREASURING* IT... UNTIL, AT LAST, MY REVERIE WAS BROKEN BY THE VOICE OF ONE OF MY *EXILES*..."

WITH THAT *CUBE* IN OUR POSSESSION ...WE SHALL RULE THE *WORLD!*

WE?? WHO DARES SPEAK OF *WE??*

THE PLAN IS *MINE!* THE CUBE IS *MINE!* THE *POWER* IS *MINE!*

AND WHAT OF *US?* ARE WE TO BE NO MORE THAN HIRED *LACKEYS??*

WE HAVE SHARED THE *DANGER!* WE MUST SHARE THE *PRIZE!*

SILENCE!! YOU ARE *NOTHING* WITHOUT ME! IT WAS *I* WHO SAVED YOU FROM *DEFEAT* WHEN THE NAZIS *FELL!*

IT IS THE *RED SKULL* WHO WAS... WHO *IS*... WHO EVER *SHALL BE* ...THE ONLY *MASTER!!*

AND, IF ANY DARE *DISPUTE* ME... *THIS* SHALL BE THEIR *FATE!*

BY THE POWER OF THE *CUBE*... I NOW TRANS-PORT YOU...

...TO THE *EDGE OF THE UNIVERSE!!*

8

HE IS *GONE!* THE CUBE IS *INFALLIBLE* AS EVER!

I CAN DO *ANY-THING!!* *ANY-THING!*

WHO DARES TO CHALLENGE ME *NOW?*

BUT... WHAT HAS *HAPPENED* TO HIM??

IS HE *LOST* TO US... *FOREVER??*

NO! NOT SO LONG AS I POSSESS THE *CUBE!*

BEHOLD!

YOU'VE BROUGHT HIM *BACK*...

WITH MERELY A *THOUGHT!!*

HE *BABBLES* INCOHERENTLY!

THAT WHICH HE HAS *SEEN*... HAS DRIVEN HIM TO THE POINT OF *MADNESS!*

NO MATTER! I CAN *RESTORE* HIS SANITY AT *ANY* TIME BY THE POWER OF THE *CUBE!*

THE SKULL IS *SUPREME!* HE MUST *EVER* BE OBEYED!

ALL HAIL THE *RED SKULL!*

...THE *REST*, MY COWED AND BEATEN FOE... IS *HISTORY!!*

ALL THAT NOW REMAINS IS... THE *FUTURE!*

AND THE FUTURE BELONGS TO THE SKULL!

9.

BUT, YOU HAVE *RESTED* LONG ENOUGH!

I AM TOO *BATTLE-WISE* NOT TO KNOW YOU WERE MERELY STALLING FOR *TIME!*

AND, SINCE IT IS *I* WHO HOLD THE *COSMIC CUBE...*

...*YOUR TIME* HAS NOW *RUN OUT!*

HE *TRANSPORTED* ME... TO ANOTHER *LAND...* ANOTHER *WORLD...* WITH JUST A *WORD!*

IS *THIS* WHERE HE INTENDS FOR ME TO MEET... MY *DEATH?*

AND, IF SO ...*HOW?*

BUT, BEFORE WE CAN *ANSWER* THAT, LET'S TURN TO *SHIELD* HQ, WHERE WE FIND A *PUZZLED RICK JONES* INTERROGATING THE GIRL CAP LOVES...

NO, RICK... I HAVEN'T *HEARD* FROM HIM!

WELL, AS FAR AS I *KNOW,* HE ISN'T SORE AT *ME...*

SO HOW COME *I* HAVEN'T *HEARD* FROM HIM?

HE'S PROBABLY STILL *HURT...* BECAUSE I WON'T QUIT *SHIELD,* AS HE *WANTS* ME TO DO!

AGENT THIRTEEN! KEEP YOUR MIND ON THIS *WEAPONRY TEST!*

10.

I'LL HEAD FOR THE *AVENGERS*...

MAYBE *THEY'VE* HAD SOME NEWS OF CAP BY NOW!

WHO'S POSTED ON *DUTY ALERT* TODAY, JARVIS?

IT'S *MR. YELLOWJACKET,* SIR...

YOU'LL FIND HIM WORKING OUT IN THE *GYMNASIUM!*

SECONDS LATER...

SORRY, YOUNGSTER... THE SHIELD-SLINGER MUST BE *GOOFING OFF* SOMEWHERE!

I DON'T *GET* IT!

NOBODY'S HEARD FROM HIM!

I DIDN'T MEAN TO SOUND SO *CALLOUS,* RICK!

STILL, COULDN'T HE JUST BE TAKING A FEW DAYS *OFF?*

BUT CAP WOULD HAVE *TOLD* ME...

OKAY IF I USE YOUR *COMMUNICHAMBER?*

YOU *KNOW* IT, SON!

I'D ALMOST *FORGOTTEN* ABOUT THE *TEEN BRIGADE*...

THE *HAM RADIO BUFFS* I USEDTA PAL AROUND WITH!

MAYBE SOME OF *THEM* CAN HELP ME NOW!

12

CALLING TEEN BRIGADE! CALLING TEEN BRIGADE!

BE ON LOOKOUT FOR *CAPTAIN AMERICA!*

RELAY ANY REPORTS TO *AVENGERS HQ,* FOR TRANSMISSION TO *RICK JONES!*

THIS IS FOR *REAL,* YOU GUYS! DON'T LET ME *DOWN!*

I GUESS I'VE *DONE* JUST ABOUT ALL I *CAN!*

THERE'S STILL JUST ONE *MORE* POSSIBILITY...BUT I'M TRYIN' TO PRETEND I NEVER EVEN *THOUGHT* OF IT...!

WHAT IF... HE JUST DOESN'T *WANT* ME... DOESN'T *NEED* ME?

WHAT IF THIS IS CAP'S WAY OF SAYIN'... *"DON'T CALL ME, RICK... I'LL CALL YOU!"*?

BUT, IF RICK JONES IS HEARTSICK *NOW*... THINK HOW HE'D FEEL IF HE KNEW THE AWFUL *TRUTH*...!

I...HAVEN'T GOT...A *CHANCE!*

SO LONG AS HE HOLDS THE *COSMIC CUBE*...

WHATEVER HE CAN *THINK* OF...MUST COME TO *PASS!*

THE SKULL CAN *CONJURE UP* NEW MENACES FASTER THAN I CAN *OVERCOME* THEM!

13

BUT, MY ATTACKS ARE STILL TOO *PETTY*...TOO *COMMONPLACE!*

THEY ARE NOT *WORTHY* OF THE ONE WHO HOLDS THE *COSMIC CUBE!*

I MUST DEVISE SOMETHING FAR MORE *UNIQUE*... FAR MORE *IMAGINATIVE* ....AS TRULY *BEFITS* THE *RED SKULL!*

I HAVE IT! AT *LAST* I KNOW THE WAY TO *BREAK* YOUR *RESOLVE*...

...THE WAY TO *CRUSH* YOUR SPIRIT... FOR *ALL TIME!*

FIRST, I MUST *WILL* YOU TO BE RESTORED TO *NORMAL SIZE*...

AND *THEN* COMES...MY *MASTER STROKE*..!

BY THE *POWER* OF THE *CUBE*... I CALL FORTH AN *IMAGE*...

I MUST LEARN THE *IDENTITY* OF THE ONE WHOM YOU MOST *LOVE*... THE ONE YOU MOST *CHERISH!*

WHAT GREATER REVENGE CAN THERE BE... THAN *THIS?*

YOU HAVE TAKEN THE *FORM* OF YOUR MOST FEARSOME *FOE*...

...WHILE ALL WHO *SEE* ME MUST NOW BELIEVE *ONE* THING...

I ALONE AM CAPTAIN AMERICA!

...JUST AS *SHE* WILL BELIEVE... AS SHE NOW *AWAKENS!*

WHAT *HAPPENED?* HOW DID I *GET* HERE?

THE *RED SKULL!!* I'VE BEEN *CAPTURED* ...BY THE *SKULL!*

IT'S *ALL RIGHT*, HONEY! HE CAN'T *HARM* YOU...

NOT WHILE *I'M* HERE TO *STOP* HIM!

SHARON! IT ISN'T *SO!* HE *ISN'T* CAPTAIN AMERICA...HE'S *ME!* HE'S *ME!!*

HOLD ME, MY DARLING! DON'T LET HIM COME ANY *CLOSER!*

THE SKULL HAS GONE *MAD!*

IT'S *HOPELESS!* THERE'S *NO WAY* THAT I CAN *CONVINCE* HER! NO WAY FOR ME TO *STOP* HIM!

BUT...WHAT WILL *HAPPEN* TO HER... AND TO ALL *MANKIND*...WHILE THE WORLD'S *DEADLIEST MENACE* CAN WALK AMONG MEN...AS *CAPTAIN AMERICA?!!*

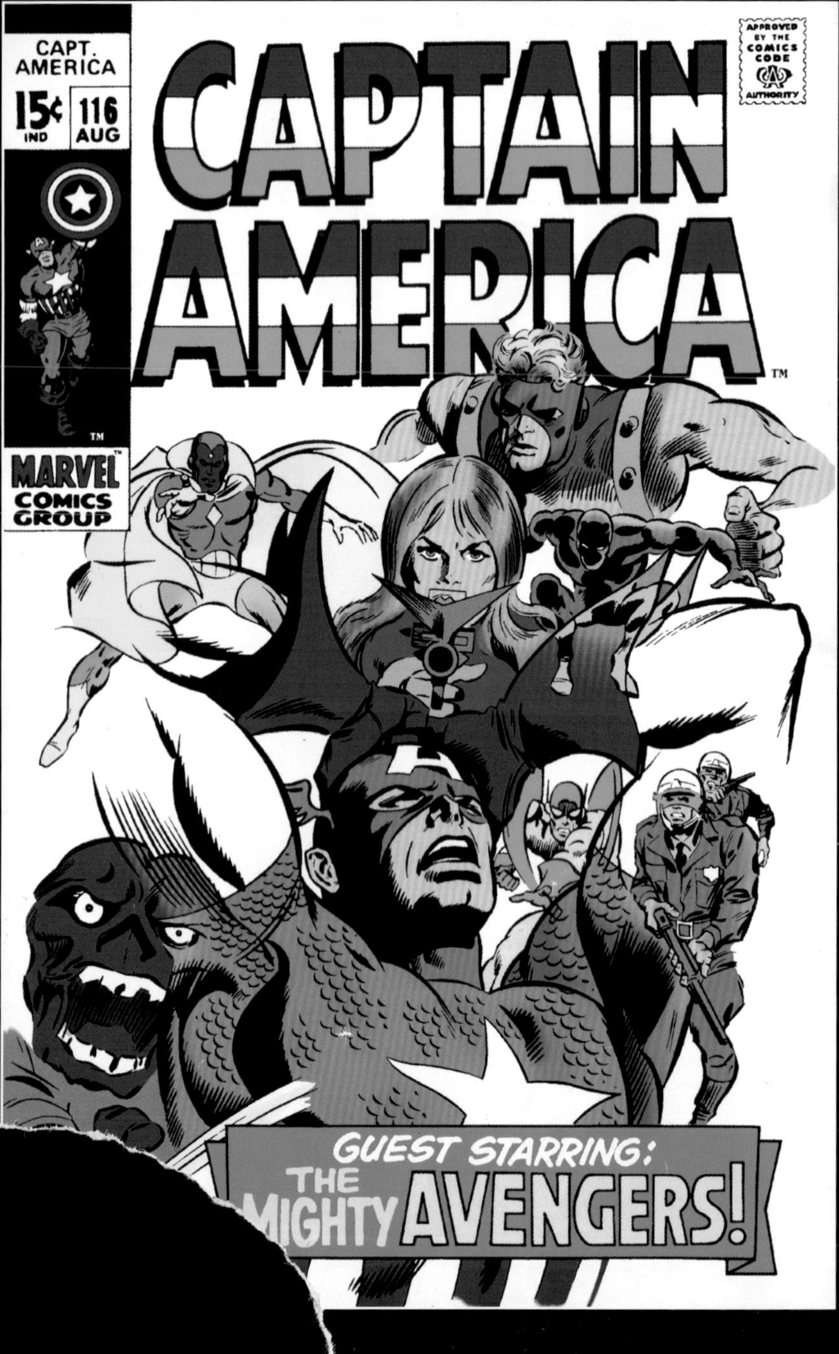

CAPT. AMERICA
15¢
IND
116
AUG
MARVEL COMICS GROUP
APPROVED BY THE COMICS CODE AUTHORITY
CAPTAIN AMERICA
GUEST STARRING:
THE MIGHTY AVENGERS!

But *we* know that the *real* Cap was hurt last ish when Sharon refused to *resign* from SHIELD at his request!

Anyway, back to our epic...

Their *relationship* is no longer any concern of *mine*!

...Since *Captain America* can never oppose me *again*!

But *now*... lest the doomed fool thinks I have *forgotten* him---

...The power of the *Cosmic Cube* shall show him *otherwise*...!

Then, at the same split-second as the *real Red Skull* merely *thinks* a random thought...

Something... is *happening* ---to me!

I'm being... *swept away*... by some strange, *invisible force*!

I've been instantaneously *transported*...to a lonely government *testing lab*!

It can only be... the doing of the *Cosmic Cube*!

TESTING LAB

But *why*? Why did the Skull *will* me here?

3.

WHATEVER HIS REASON... HE'S PROBABLY *WATCHING* ME RIGHT *NOW!*

...ENJOY- ING THE FACT THAT SO LONG AS I'VE TAKEN ON *HIS* *APPEARANCE!*

I'M IN DANGER OF BEING *SHOT ON SIGHT!*

AND, AS THOUGH TO *PROVE* THE TRUTH OF THE DESPERATE AVENGER'S WORDS...

HARRY!... LOOK!! OVER THERE... BEHIND THAT *TREE..!*

I'D KNOW 'IM *ANYWHERE...*

IT'S THE *RED SKULL!*

THEY *SEE* ME! I'VE GOT TO *RUN* FOR IT!

STOP! STOP...OR WE'LL *SHOOT!*

TO *ANY* ALERT, ARMED *GUARD*... THE SIGHT OF THE *RED SKULL,* AT A PLACE LIKE *THIS...* CAN ONLY MEAN *ONE* THING!

ALL THE *DEFEATS* I'VE SUFFERED AT THE HANDS OF CAPTAIN AMERICA ARE AS *NOTHING...* COMPARED TO THE INEXPRESSIBLE, INDESCRIBABLE *TRAP OF DEATH* INTO WHICH I HAVE HURLED HIM!

BUT, IT'S NOT *ENOUGH!*

THE GUARDS MAY YET *HOLD* THEIR FIRE!

I MUST MAKE *CERTAIN* THAT HIS *DOOM* IS SEALED!

THUS, ONCE *AGAIN,* THE INFALLIBLE *COSMIC CUBE* SHALL DO MY BIDDING...!

4

AND, EVEN AS THE *SKULL* PREPARES HIS *NEXT* MIRACULOUS MOVE...

KRAK!

DON'T TAKE ANY *CHANCES* WITH 'IM! HE'S ONE OF THE MOST *DANGEROUS* MEN ALIVE!

I WAS A *FOOL* TO RUN! I *RATTLED* THEM SO...THEY'D RATHER *FIRE* THAN FACE ME!

I *THOUGHT* I HEARD SHOOTING! THAT'S THE *RED SKULL* OUT THERE!

HE MUST BE AFTER OUR *NEW DEVICES!*

QUICK! THROW THE *EMERGENCY* SWITCH... IT'LL SLIDE OUR UNIT *BELOW* GROUND LEVEL!

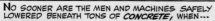

NO SOONER ARE THE MEN AND MACHINES SAFELY LOWERED BENEATH TONS OF *CONCRETE,* WHEN...

BUHR

OOM!

5

DIDJA SEE *THAT?* HALF OF THE *INSTALLATION*---WENT UP IN *SMOKE!*

NO! IT WASN'T *ME!* I HAD NOTHING TO *DO* WITH IT!

SURE---SURE! IT WAS THE BAD OL' WICKED *WITCH* WHO DID IT!

SO *THAT'S* WHAT THE SKULL WAS *UP* TO!

CAN'T LET THEM TAKE ME *IN!* THEN THERE'LL BE NO*BODY* LEFT TO SUSPECT THE *REAL* SKULL!

I MAY BE IN THE WRONG *BODY*...

BUT I STILL HAVE MY OLD *BATTLE SKILL!*

ZZK

SORRY, ABOUT THIS, MEN!

BUT THERE'S *MORE* AT STAKE THAN JUST YOU AND *ME*...

AND THERE'S *NO WAY* I CAN *CONVINCE* YOU RIGHT *NOW!*

THERE'S ONLY *ONE* THING IN MY FAVOR..!

THE SKULL IS PROBABLY *ENJOYING* THIS TOO MUCH TO WANT IT TO *END!*

SO LONG AS HE HOLDS THE *CUBE*, HE FEELS I'M *DOOMED*...

SO HE'D RATHER KEEP GIVING ME ENOUGH *ROPE*... THAN *FINISH* ME RIGHT NOW!

AND THAT'S JUST THE WAY I *WANT* IT!

SO LONG AS I'M *ALIVE*... I'VE GOT A *CHANCE*, NO MATTER HOW SMALL!

SOONER OR LATER...HE MAY MAKE *ONE* SLIP... AND WHEN HE *DOES*...

THE *REAL* CAPTAIN AMERICA WILL *FIGHT*... AS NEVER BEFORE!

AN EMPTY *CAR!* JUST WHAT I *NEED!*

6

[117]

YOU CAN *INTERCEPT* HIM ON *ROUTE 104,* LONGRIDGE ROAD... HEADING TOWARDS THE *MERRITT PARKWAY!*

HOW DO YOU *KNOW,* CAP?

IF I *TOLD* YOU, I DOUBT YOU'D *BELIEVE* IT!

...WHICH IS POSSIBLY THE *UNDERSTATEMENT* OF THE CENTURY!

WITHIN A MATTER OF SECONDS, THE *ALL-POINTS BULLETIN* IS RADIOED THRUOUT THE EASTERN STATES....AS THE NET DRAWS *TIGHTER* AROUND THE DESPERATELY FLEEING AVENGER...

INTERCEPT RED SKULL !!!

EVEN THOUGH *EVERYTHING* IS AGAINST ME...

EVEN THOUGH I HAVE ANOTHER MAN'S *FACE* AND HIS *FORM*...

EVEN THOUGH HE POSSESSES THE INVINCIBLE *COSMIC CUBE*...

I *HAVE* TO KEEP *TRYING*... TO KEEP *FIGHTING*...

IT'S THE *ONLY* WAY I *KNOW!*

A *BARRICADE*... THROWN ACROSS THE ROAD!

I *SWERVED* JUST IN TIME, TO *MISS* IT!

IT'S A *ROAD BLOCK* ...AND THEY'VE *SPOTTED* ME!

8

CAN'T STOP NOW! I'LL *NEVER* BE ABLE TO PROVE WHAT'S *HAPPENED* TO ME IF I'M THROWN BEHIND *BARS!*

MY ONLY CHANCE IS TOTAL *SURPRISE!*

THEY'LL *NEVER* EXPECT ME TO HEAD FOR THAT *EMBANKMENT!*

...WHICH IS *JUST* WHAT I'VE GOT TO *DO!*

B-YOW

SPTWEEEE

IF I CAN MAINTAIN ENOUGH *SPEED*... THE *CENTRIFUGAL FORCE* WILL KEEP ME FROM *FALLING*...

...UNTIL I CAN RACE DOWN *BEHIND* THEM!

SKREEEEEE

9.

SPANG!

MADE IT!

BUT I'M NOT OUT OF THE WOODS YET!

I'VE GOT A *HEAD START* ON THEM FOR *NOW*...

BUT THEY'RE SURE TO RADIO *AHEAD* OF ME...AT THE NEXT HIGHWAY *TOLL STATION!*

STILL, THERE'S NOTHING I CAN *DO* ABOUT IT! I'VE *GOT* TO KEEP GOING!

WHEN I THINK OF *SHARON* ...TRUSTING THAT---

NO! NO! I HAVE TO PUT IT... OUT OF MY *MIND!*

RADIO FOR ANOTHER *ROAD BLOCK* AT TOLL BOOTH FIVE!

MEANWHILE, WE'LL TAKE OFF AND TRY TO *NAB* HIM!

LOOK *SHARP*, BILL...THAT CREEP'S A *KILLER!*

THAT'S *WHY* HE MUSTN'T GET *AWAY!*

WEEEEEE

I STILL DON'T *GET* IT!

WHY WOULD THE *SKULL* PUT HIMSELF OUT ON A *LIMB* LIKE THIS?

FROM ALL I'VE *READ* ABOUT 'IM, IT'S JUST NOT HIS *STYLE!*

POLICE STAMFORD

YOU'RE *RIGHT*, MAC! HE'S USUALLY GOT A POCKET-SIZED *ARMY* BACKING HIM UP!

...WITH A DOZEN *ESCAPE ROUTES* ALL WORKED OUT IN ADVANCE!

WELL, IF HE WANTS TO CHANGE HIS TACTICS, IT'S NO SKIN OFF *OUR* NOSES!

10.

GET *SET!* HERE HE *COMES!*

DOESN'T LOOK LIKE HE PLANS TO *STOP!*

HE'S *GOT* TO STOP! HE'S GOT NO *CHOICE!*

BUT THE MAN BEHIND THE WHEEL OF THE MADLY-HURTLING CAR THINKS *DIFFERENTLY...*

IT'S *WORTH* A CHANCE! THERE'S ONLY *ONE* CAR IN THE OTHER LANE!

NOW!

KADOM

KRAK!

SPANG!

TOLL

MADE IT!

KLLANNG!

NOW! IF I CAN JUST REACH A *SIDE ROAD* IN TIME!

PTWEE

12

MEANWHILE, AT THE WORLD-FAMOUS HEADQUARTERS OF THE MIGHTY AVENGERS...

IF IT'S ALL THE SAME TO YOU GENTS...

I'D RATHER BE WATCHING JULIA!

I DON'T LIKE IT! THE RED SKULL IS HEADING THIS WAY!

WHAT'S THE BIG DEAL?

WE OUGHTTA BE ABLE TO TAKE 'IM!

THAT'S NOT THE POINT!

WHAT'S HAPPENED TO CAP? WHY ISN'T HE AFTER HIM?

THAT'S WHAT I'VE BEEN SAYING...!

THERE'S GOTTA BE A REASON WHY WE HAVEN'T HEARD FROM HIM YET!

AND I'M GONNA FIND OUT WHAT IT IS!

WATCH OUT FOR THE SKULL, RICK!

DON'T TRY TO FACE HIM ALONE!

THEY STILL THINK I'M TOO YOUNG TO BE MUCH HELP TO ANYONE!

WELL, I'LL JUST PROVE HOW WRONG THEY ARE!

AND THIS IS AS GOOD A TIME AS ANY TO START!

13.

GET *OUT* OF HERE! IF I *NEED* YOU, I'LL *SEND* FOR YOU!

AND DON'T HOLD YOUR BREATH *WAITING!*

HE..HE NEVER *TALKED* TO ME...!

GOOD *RIDDANCE!*

I DO NOT LIKE MY *REVERIES* TO BE DISTURBED!

AH! MY UNWILLING *VICTIM* APPROACHES THE HEAD-QUARTERS OF...THE *AVENGERS!*

AND I'LL NEVER GIVE 'IM THE *CHANCE*... TO DO IT *AGAIN!*

SORRY, CAP...SORRY THAT I *BOTHERED* YOU!

GUESS I WAS A *FOOL*... TO THINK A GUY LIKE *ME*... COULD FILL THE SHOES OF *BUCKY BARNES!*

DOESN'T HE *KNOW* WE HAVE AN ELECTRONIC *VIDEO SENTRY* SYSTEM?

HEADS UP, AVENGERS!

HE'S HEADING FOR THE *GYM!*

I'LL BET I COULD TAKE 'IM *ALONE*... WITHOUT CHANGING *SIZE!*

MAYBE SO! BUT IT COULD BE A *TRICK!*

WE'D BETTER FACE HIM AT *FULL STRENGTH!*

OKAY, YJ---THEN EVERYONE *STAND BACK*..!

IT'S A *LONG SHOT*... BUT MAYBE *PYM*, OR *STARK*, OR *ANY* OF THEM CAN FIND AN *ANTIDOTE* FOR WHAT'S *HAPPENED* TO ME!

THAT IS... IF THEY CAN BE *CONVINCED* OF WHO I REALLY *AM!*

GYM

15

IT IS *DONE!* WHEN HE REGAINS *CONSCIOUSNESS,* HE IS CERTAIN TO BE FAR MORE *DOCILE!*

BUT-- *WAIT!* THE LOUDSPEAKER SUMMONS US!

ATTENTION, *AVENGERS!* REPORT TO *SHIELD! URGENT! URGENT!*

THAT'S *IT!* PLAY TIME'S *OVER!*

TIE HIM *UP* TILL WE *RETURN!*

I'LL CLUE *JARVIS* IN ON WHAT HAPPENED--- JUST IN CASE!

WELL, WELL, WELL! SO THE *AVENGERS* HAVE CAPTURED THE BIG, BAD *RED SKULL!*

BUT, I CAN'T JUST LET HIM *LIE* THERE--- THAT WOULD BE TOO *DULL!*

I'LL WILL HIS *LADY LOVE* TO VISIT THE BUILDING...

---BECAUSE I'VE FINALLY *DECIDED* HOW MY ACCURSED FOE SHALL *DIE!*

HOW *INGENIOUS* IT WILL BE ...IF HE *PERISHES* AT THE HAND OF THE ONE WHO *LOVES* HIM MOST!

NO, MA'AM... *CAPTAIN AMERICA* HAS NOT RETURNED!

THE *SKULL?* THEN I MUST *SEE* HIM...AT *ONCE!*

BUT THE AVENGERS HAVE MADE THE *RED SKULL* THEIR *CAPTIVE!*

19.

CAPT. AMERICA
15¢ IND
117 SEPT
APPROVED BY THE COMICS CODE AUTHORITY
CAPTAIN AMERICA
TM
THE COMING OF THE FALCON!
MARVEL COMICS GROUP

AN *ISLAND*... LONELY AND DESOLATE... SOMEWHERE IN THE *TROPICS!*

IT MUST BE ONE OF THE *MANY* REMOTE AREAS WHERE THE SKULL HAS HIDDEN *BASES!*

EVEN AS I *LAND* HERE... I CAN ALMOST *FEEL* HIS EYES UPON ME...

HE'S *WATCHING*... *SCHEMING*... *REVELLING* IN MY HELPLESS-NESS!

BUT *LET* THE MADMAN GLOAT... WHILE HE *CAN!*

SOONER OR LATER, HE'S BOUND TO MAKE A *SLIP*...

AND WHEN HE *DOES*... I'LL BE READY AND WAITING ...TO *STRIKE BACK!*

2.

HE HASN'T *YET* LOST FAITH! WHY CAN'T I CRUSH HIS *SPIRIT?*

BUT, NO MATTER! NOT EVEN HIS INDOMITABLE *WILL* CAN SAVE HIM *NOW!*

NOTHING CAN SAVE HIM...FROM THOSE WHO ARE *COMING!*

I HEAR *VOICES...* COMING *CLOSER...* IN THE DISTANCE!

THE ACCURSED *SKULL* THOUGHT HE HAD SEEN THE *LAST* OF US WHEN HE *MAROONED* US UPON THIS BARREN ISLE!

BUT SOON WE SHALL BE *FREE* OF THIS WRETCHED PLACE ...FREE TO SEEK OUR DEADLY *REVENGE!*

THERE IS NO PLACE ON *EARTH* WHERE HE CAN HIDE FROM US!

NO PLACE ON *EARTH* WHERE HE CAN BE SAFE ...WHERE THE SKULL CAN *ESCAPE* THE COMBINED POWER OF ---*THE EXILES!*

3.

IT WAS *WE* WHO FOUND THE ALL-MIGHTY *COSMIC CUBE!*

IT IS *WE* WHO MUST SHARE ITS SUPREME, EARTH-SHATTERING *POWER!*

THE SKULL WILL NOT *ESCAPE* US!

AND SHARE IT WE *SHALL,* CADAVUS! SO WE HAVE *SWORN!*

ONLY THE RED SKULL'S *DEATH* CAN GIVE US OUR TOTAL *TRIUMPH!*

SO *THAT'S* WHY HE SENT ME TO THIS SPOT!

IF THEY *FIND* ME...I'M *DONE* FOR!

THE *TREE...* SHAKING LOOSE FROM *BENEATH* ME!

IT'S *MORE* OF HIS DOING! HE'S STILL *WATCHING!* HE *WILLED* IT!

LOOK! FALLING FROM THE UNDERBRUSH ...*AHEAD* OF US...!

THEY *SEE* ME!

4.

HE DOESN'T *REALIZE* THAT WE'VE BOTH FOUGHT *BEFORE!*

I REMEMBER BALDINI'S *SKILL*...AND HIS *WEAKNESS!*

AT THE INSTANT HIS SCARF MAKES *CONTACT*...

HE MUST *LOOSEN* HIS GRIP... FOR TOTAL *MOBILITY!*

AND, AT THAT VERY SPLIT-SECOND...

...*I STRIKE!*

I SHALL FINISH HIM...WITH A *SINGLE* SHOT!

NO, CHANG!

SHOOO,SST!

MY *MURDER CHAIR* WILL DO IT *BETTER!*

I WAS *READY* FOR THAT ONE!

BUT HOW *LONG* CAN I KEEP DODGING HIS INEXHAUSTIBLE *BLASTS?*

6

WHAT A MAGNIFICENT STROKE OF SHEER *GENIUS* ON MY PART!

NOT ONLY WILL HE *DIE*... BUT HE WILL FALL IN THE *GUISE* OF HIS MOST HATED *FOE!*

NO NEED TO WATCH HIS *FINAL MOMENTS*...

SUCH SORDID SIGHTS *DEPRESS* ME!

AND, THERE IS STILL A *WORLD* FOR ME TO WIN!

BUT, EVEN AS THE *REAL* SKULL TURNS TRIUMPHANTLY AWAY...

HAUPTMANN... *LOOK OUT!*

A *FALCON!* IF...THOSE *CLAWS* HAD STRUCK MY *FACE*...!

HE TURNED *AWAY!*

IF I CAN LASH OUT *FAST* ENOUGH...

8.

[139]

HE'S *LEAVING*...LIKE SOMEONE WHO KNOWS THAT HIS JOB IS *DONE!*

THIS GROTESQUE *SKULL FACE* IS REALLY JUST A *MASK!*

BUT THEY'LL BE *SEARCHING* FOR ME AGAIN IN *MINUTES!* I STILL HAVE TO...

SAY! I JUST REALIZED SOMETHING...!

CHANCES ARE...THE *EXILES* HAVE NEVER EVEN *SEEN* THE FACE BENEATH!

SO, IF I JUST *REMOVE* IT...

I SHOULD HAVE THOUGHT OF THIS *LONG* AGO!

I WOULDN'T HAVE HAD TO WORRY ABOUT THE *POLICE*... OR ANYONE!

NOBODY WOULD EVER RECOGNIZE THE SKULL WITHOUT HIS *MASK!*

AND YET... WHAT IF THE EXILES *HAVE* SEEN HIS FACE!

I CAN'T AFFORD TO *CHANCE* IT!

BUT, IF I CAN USE THIS *CLAY* PROPERLY...I WON'T *HAVE* TO...

IT'LL FURNISH A PERFECT *BASE* FOR A MAKESHIFT *DISGUISE!*

10.

MEANWHILE, BACK IN NEW YORK---

STARE, YOU FOOLS! STARE AT YOUR HERO, CAPTAIN AMERICA!

LITTLE DO YOU DREAM THAT MY EXILES HAVE ALREADY WRITTEN FINIS TO HIS MISERABLE CAREER!

BUT I AM NOT SOME COSTUMED ODDITY... SOME COLORFUL FREAK TO BE GAPED AT BY THE UNDESERVING MASSES!

TAXI! WAIT!

CAPTAIN AMERICA?!!

HEY, I THOUGHT YOU GUYS JUST KINDA FLEW THRU THE AIR!

THERE IS NO NEED TO THINK! JUST DRIVE!

THE GRINNING, WAVING, SIMPERING PUBLIC! HOW I DESPISE IT!

IF ONLY THEY KNEW...AS I BENIGNLY SMILE AT THEM...

THEY SOON SHALL BE MY HELPLESS SLAVES!

FOR, SO LONG AS THE COSMIC CUBE IS MINE---

THERE IS NOTHING BEYOND THE GRASP OF THE RED SKULL!

AND IT SHALL BE MINE... FOREVER!

RAD CITY

KIRK DOUGLAS

BROTHERHOOD

11.

I HAVE NO **MONEY** WITH ME...BUT IF YOU WILL GIVE ME YOUR NAME AND ADDRESS...

THAT'S OKAY, CAP! IT'S A **PLEASURE** TO GIVE A GUY LIKE **YOU** A FREE RIDE! JUST **FORGET** IT, PAL!

PRECISELY WHAT I **INTEND** TO DO, YOU HERO- WORSHIPPING **SIMPLETON!**

LOOK! ACROSS THE STREET! IT'S **CAPTAIN AMERICA!** HE MUST BE REGISTERING AT THE **HOTEL!** HOW **ABOUT** THAT!

WELL, I GUESS HE'S GOTTA BED DOWN **SOMEWHERE!**

STRANGE...I NEVER THOUGHT CAPTAIN AMERICA WOULD **SWAGGER** SO!

ALMOST AS IF HE **REVELS** IN THE ATTENTION OF THE PUBLIC!

CAPTAIN AMERICA! ARE YOU GOING TO BE STAYING **HERE?**

WHY **NOT?** ISN'T IT THE **BEST** HOTEL IN TOWN?

FEEL HIS **MUSCLES,** GALS! IT'LL MAKE A GREAT **PIC!**

OHHH!

ENJOY IT WHILE YOU **MAY,** MY DEAR!

FOR SOON YOU WILL **BOW** TO ME, INSTEAD!

CLICK!

CLICK!!

CLICK!

TAKE **ALL** THE PICTURES YOU WISH!

FOR, LITTLE DO YOU **DREAM** THAT YOU ARE MERELY PERPETUATING THE SHALLOW MEMORY OF...A **DEAD** MAN!

12.

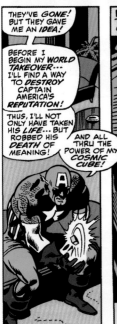

*ADVANCED IDEA MECHANICS...THE EVIL SECRET SOCIETY WHO *CREATED* THE COSMIC CUBE! ... STAN.

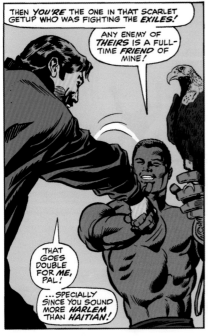

[147]

MINUTES LATER---

THIS USED TO BE A HAPPY *VILLAGE*... UNTIL THE *EXILES* CAME!

THE NATIVES WERE *PEACEFUL* --- DIDN'T EVEN HAVE A *POPGUN* BETWEEN THEM...

SO IT WASN'T LONG BEFORE THEY WERE TURNED INTO *SERFS* BY THEIR NEW, WELL-ARMED *MASTERS*!

I'VE BEEN TRYING TO *ORGANIZE* THEM... BAND THEM TOGETHER AND GET THEM TO *FIGHT* FOR THE FREEDOM THAT THEY'VE LOST!

BUT, IT'S AN *UP-HILL* JOB!

IT WOULD *HAVE* TO BE!

THE EXILES ARE PROFESSIONAL *KILLERS*!

BUT WHAT ABOUT *YOU*? WHO *ARE* YOU? WHAT'S *YOUR* STAKE IN ALL THIS?

I'VE BEEN *WONDERING* ABOUT THAT MYSELF! IT'S KINDA *FUNNY* HOW IT ALL HAPPENED---

EVER SINCE I CAN *REMEMBER*, I'VE BEEN *NUTS* ABOUT BIRDS!

I USED TO HAVE THE BIGGEST *PIGEON COOP* ON ANY ROOFTOP IN HARLEM!

MAN! I COULD PRACTICALLY MAKE THOSE HIGH-FLYERS *TALK!*

BUT THEN--- I GOT ALL HUNG UP ON *FALCONS*..!

17.

"IT STARTED IN *RIO*...WHERE I WENT FOR A *VACATION*..."

"THE FIRST TIME I *SAW* ONE...I WAS *HOOKED*...BUT FOR *GOOD!*"

"THEN, I FINALLY FOUND *REDWING*...AND BOUGHT HIM FOR MY *OWN!*"

"WE'VE GOT SOMETHING *GOIN'* FOR US THAT NO-BODY ELSE COULD UNDERSTAND--!"

"HE'S *MORE* THAN A *BIRD!* MORE THAN A *FALCON!* IT'S LIKE...HE'S A *PART* OF ME!"

WELL, TO MAKE A LONG STORY SHORT, I ANSWERED AN *AD* IN THE PAPER...

IT WAS FROM THE *EXILES*...BUT I DIDN'T *KNOW* THEM AT THE TIME!

THEY WERE *BORED*...LOOK-ING FOR *KICKS!* THEY WANTED TO HIRE A *HUNTING FALCON!*

SO, REDWING AND ME HOPPED THE FIRST *FREIGHTER* ...AND HERE WE *ARE!*

18

BUT, WHEN I SAW WHAT A *SUCKER PLAY* I'D MADE...WE *CUT OUT*...BUT *FAST!*

THE *EXILES* DON'T HIRE *WORKERS...*

THEY JUST KEEP *PRISONERS!*

YOU SAID SOMETHING BEFORE ...ABOUT ORGANIZING THE *OTHERS* HERE... TO FIGHT *BACK...!*

HOW DO YOU PLAN TO *DO* IT, WITHOUT ANY WEAPONS?

WE'LL *MAKE* WEAPONS! OUT OF *STICKS 'N STONES* IF WE HAVE TO!

ANY-THING'S BETTER THAN NOT FIGHTING BACK!

AFTER THE WAY I SAW *YOU* HANDLE YOURSELF BACK THERE...

I'M KINDA HOPING YOU'LL TOSS *IN* WITH ME!

YOU COULDN'T *STOP* ME, FRIEND!

BUT IT'LL TAKE *MORE* THAN GUTS! THEY'VE GOT THE ARMS... *YOU'LL* NEED A *GIMMICK!*

YEAH? LIKE *WHAT?*

I THINK I'VE *GOT IT...!*

YOU NEED SOME-THING TO SERVE AS A *SYMBOL* TO THE NATIVES...

AND SOMETHING THAT'LL *UNNERVE* THE EXILES....MAKE THEM *WONDER* WHO THEY'RE FIGHTING!

A *MASK* AND *COSTUME* OUGHT TO DO IT...TOGETHER WITH A STIRRING *NAME*...LIKE, FOR INSTANCE... *THE FALCON!*

ME, A COSTUMED CLOWN?

DON'T PUT ME *ON,* MAN!

DON'T *KNOCK* IT, FELLA! IT'S BEEN KNOWN TO *WORK!*

AND *I'M* THE GUY TO SHOW YOU *HOW!*

19

CAPT. AMERICA

15¢ 118 OCT

APPROVED BY THE COMICS CODE AUTHORITY

MARVEL COMICS GROUP

CAPTAIN AMERICA

THE FALCON FIGHTS!

CAPTAIN AMERICA, LIVING LEGEND of WORLD WAR II ™

THE FALCON FIGHTS ON!

THE TRIUMPHANT *RED SKULL* HAS USED THE POWER OF HIS *COSMIC CUBE* TO CHANGE BODIES WITH *CAPTAIN AMERICA!* NOW, ON A FAR-OFF ISLE, THE DEADLY *EXILES* HUNT OUR HERO!...AND SO WE BEGIN...

SCRIPT: STAN LEE...ART: GENE COLAN... INKING: JOE SINNOTT...LETTERING: SAM ROSEN

THE *EXILES* WERE TRAINED BY ME *PERSONALLY* TO BE THE MOST RUTHLESS, MOST *BLOODTHIRSTY* OF ALL!

AND YET, THEY *STILL* HAVEN'T CAUGHT THEIR QUARRY!

BUT THE ISLE IS SO *SMALL*... AND *NO ONE* COULD MISTAKE THE *RED SKULL!*

WHY HAVEN'T THEY *CAUGHT* HIM? *WHY??*

NOT EVEN THE *EXILES* HAVE EVER SEEN THE WAY I *REALLY* LOOK!

BUT *WAIT!* THE ONE THING I DIDN'T *THINK* OF... WHAT IF HE TOOK *OFF* MY RED SKULL *MASK?*

2.

IF HE HID MY RED *JUMP-SUIT* AND WENT WITHOUT MY *MASK*, HE COULD PROBABLY *AVOID* THEM FOR *DAYS!*

BUT HE *STILL* CANNOT ESCAPE THEM...

---FOR THERE'S NO WAY *OFF* THE ISLAND!

THEREFORE, I'LL LET THEM *CONTINUE* THEIR SEARCH ---WITHOUT INTERFERING!

AFTER ALL, I HAVE *NOTHING* TO LOSE!

SO LONG AS THE ALL-POWERFUL *CUBE* IS MINE, NO ONE CAN *EVER* DEFY ME!

AND THE CUBE WILL BE MINE... *FOREVER!*

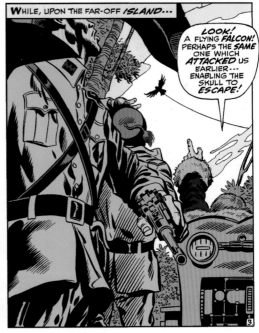

*W*HILE, UPON THE FAR-OFF *ISLAND*...

LOOK! A FLYING *FALCON!* PERHAPS THE *SAME* ONE WHICH *ATTACKED* US EARLIER --- ENABLING THE SKULL TO *ESCAPE!*

STAND BACK! THE ACCURSED BIRD WILL *BOTHER* US NO MORE!

KRAK!

KRAK! KRAK!

YOU *MISSED* HIM, YOU *BUNGLER!*

KRAK KRAK

KRAK KRAK K

KRAK

KRAK

GUNSHOTS! SOMEONE'S FIRING AT *REDWING!*

DON'T *WORRY*, MISTER! ONLY THE EXILE NAMED *CHING* CARRIES A GUN...

AND, SINCE IT'S MERELY A *PISTOL*, IT WON'T BE HARD FOR YOUR HUNTING HAWK TO SOAR OUT OF *RANGE!*

4

YOU WERE **RIGHT!** HERE HE **COMES!**

HE'S A **GREAT** BIRD, FELLA! YOU'VE REALLY TRAINED HIM **WELL!**

YOU **KNOW** IT, MAN! REDWING AND **ME,** WE'RE A **TEAM!** AIN'T **NOTHIN'** WE CAN'T DO TOGETHER!

YEP, IT'S **STILL** KINDA HARD TO BELIEVE! HERE AM I... **SAM WILSON,** FROM THE SWINGIN' SLUMS OF **HARLEM, U.S.A....**

STUCK ON A **HIDDEN ISLAND** IN THE MIDDLE OF NOWHERE... WITH SOME NUT WHO'S GONNA MAKE A **SUPERHERO** OF ME!

STRANGER THINGS HAVE HAPPENED, SAM! YOU'VE ALL THE **EQUIPMENT** YOU NEED!

YOU'VE **BRAINS, BRAWN,** AND A ONE-IN-A-MILLION **BIRD!**

OKAY, THEN... GET OUT OF THOSE THREADS AND INTO YOUR **COSTUME!**

KNOW SOMETHIN', PAL? THE **CRAZIEST** PART ABOUT THE DEAL IS... I'M **BUYIN'** IT!

WE'VE GOT SOME **TRAINING** TO DO!

AND SO...

YOUR MOVE, FALCON! ATTACK ME!

HARDER! DON'T PULL BACK!

YOU GAVE ME TIME TO BLOCK YOUR RIGHT ARM! THAT'S BAD!

AND SEE HOW I KEEP YOUR LEFT HAND OUT OF ACTION?

HOW'D YOU EVER BECOME SUCH A ONE-MAN ARMY?

NEVER MIND ABOUT THAT, FRIEND!

NOTICE HOW I SHIFT MY WEIGHT, USING MY HIP TO SWING YOU OFF-BALANCE...!

THAT'S IT... IF YOU MUST FALL, LOOSEN UP... LET YOUR SHOULDER TAKE THE IMPACT!

DON'T GET DISCOURAGED, SAM!

YOU CAN'T HOPE TO ABSORB IN A FEW LESSONS WHAT TOOK ME A LIFETIME TO LEARN!

BUT YOU'VE GOT STYLE, FELLA! YOU'LL BE OKAY!

HEY, WITH A TEACHER LIKE YOU, I'LL BE THE GREATEST!

HOW CAN I MISS?

6

HOUR AFTER HOUR, THE GRUEL-LING SESSION *CONTINUES*...

AND, WITH EACH NEW ASSAULT, EACH NEW *MANEUVER*, THE FALCON SEEMS TO GROW *SWIFTER*... *SURER*... *STRONGER*!

GOOD WORK, SAM! YOUR TIMING WAS *PERFECT*!

BUT REMEMBER YOUR *FOLLOW-THRU*! DON'T LOSE THE *INITIATIVE*!

THAT'S IT! YOU'RE A *NATURAL* AT KARATE!

KNOW SOMETHIN', MAN? AFTER FIGHTIN' ALL THOSE *STREET GANGS* BACK HOME, THIS IS JUST LIKE *OLD TIMES* TO SAM WILSON!

FORGET SAM WILSON! YOU'RE THE *FALCON* NOW!

WHEN YOU WEAR THAT *COSTUME*, YOU EAT, DRINK, AND *BREATHE* THE FALCON!

7.

I could *dispose* of that liberty-loving *clod* with just a random *thought*...

But why make it easy for the *exiles*?

Let them spend their time hunting, searching...

The *phone!* At *this* hour?

PRING

It will be *amusing* to see the kind of call that *Captain America* might receive so early in the morning!

What is that? You dare intrude upon my *privacy* for so trifling a matter?!!

I can't *help* it, sir! The lobby is *crawling* with your *fans!*

They started arriving before *dawn!* I don't think we can hold them *off* very much *longer!*

Give a *yell!* Give a *yap!* Give a *cheer* for ol' *cap!*

Perhaps if you came down and *spoke* to them...?

8

[160]

FLOORS 2-10

C'MON! EVERYBODY UP!

THE FIFTH FLOOR ...AND HURRY!

THE LOATHESOME AMERICAN *SHEEP!* I CAN NOT *STOMACH* THEM!

I'LL JUST USE THE CUBE TO *EVADE* THEM WITH EASE!

WAIT! HOLD IT! YOU *CAN'T!*

GET *WITH* IT, GUY! OL' *CAP* IS UP THERE... IN LIVING COLOR!

CAP...WAIT! WE CAME UP TO *TALK* TO YOU!

FOOLS! WHAT CAN *I* HAVE TO SAY... TO THE LIKES OF *YOU?!!*

BUT, WHAT OF THE HEARTSICK *YOUTH* WHO HAD HOPED TO REPLACE THE LONG-GONE *BUCKY BARNES* AS CAP'S FIGHTING PARTNER? WHAT OF THE LONELY, SILENTLY-BROODING *RICK JONES*--?

THE *LAST* TIME...I SAW CAP...

HE ACTED ...LIKE I WAS...A *STRANGER* TO HIM!

WELL...*OKAY!* I DON'T NEED A *HOUSE* TO FALL ON ME!

SO I'M *NOT* ANOTHER BUCKY... *BIG DEAL!*

MAYBE THIS IS WHERE I *GROW UP*... WHERE I STOP TRYIN' TO LIVE SOME *OTHER* JOE'S LIFE!

R.I.P.!

SO LONG, AVENGER...

MAYBE WE'LL GET TOGETHER SOME DAY, JUST FOR LAUGHS...

BUT... DON'T HOLD YOUR BREATH WAITING!

NOTE: FOR THE *SURPRISE* OF THE SEASON, SEE WHAT FATE HAS IN STORE FOR RICK IN *CAPTAIN MARVEL #17,* NOW ON SALE! BUT NOW...*ONWARD*...

12.

REMEMBER LAST ISH WHEN WE TOOK YOU TO THE HEADQUARTERS OF *AIM**? WELL, LET'S *RECHECK* THE PROGRESS OF THEIR MOST *FANTASTIC* EXPERIMENT...

WE MUST WORK *FASTER*, OR MIGHTY *MODOK* WILL BE DISPLEASED!

THE ALL-POWERFUL *CUBE* HAS BEEN *STOLEN* FROM US...

BUT IT MUST *NEVER* BE USED BY ANY *OTHER*!

THEREFORE ITS POWER MUST BE *DESTROYED*!

*AIM: ADVANCED IDEA MECHANICS... THE MYSTERIOUS MASTERMINDS WHO *CREATED* THE COSMIC CUBE!...STAN.

AND DESTROYED IT *SHALL* BE... OR WE'LL ANSWER TO *MODOK* WITH OUR VERY *LIVES*!

NOW...*STAND BACK!* FOR *THIS* IS OUR MOMENT OF TRUTH!

EVERYTHING DEPENDS UPON WHETHER THE CATHOLITE BLOCK WILL *CHANGE SHAPE!*...

WE'VE *DONE* IT! THE BLOCK IS NOW *ROUND!*

THUS, ALL THAT REMAINS IS... *PHASE THREE!*

13.

BUT TO RESCUE OUR TALE FROM SUCH TOTAL *CONFUSION*, LET'S ALL CLEAR OUR HEADS WITH SOME *ACTION*---

LOOK! IT'S THE *EXILES!*

DO YOU FEEL UP TO *TACKLING* THEM, FALCON?

SO WE NOW COME TO GRIPS ...AT *LAST!*

JUST *WATCH* ME AND SEE!

I'VE TAUGHT YOU ALL I *CAN*, FRIEND! HERE'S WHERE IT PAYS *OFF!*

THEN WHAT ARE WE *WAITING* FOR, MAN?

LET'S.. ..GO!

14

THEY'RE BOTH *UNARMED!* WHAT *CHANCE* CAN THEY HAVE?

SPOK!

WHEN YOU'RE HOOKED ON *HUNTING FALCONS...*

YOU BEGIN TO DEVELOP AN *INSTINCT...* ALMOST AS GOOD AS *THEIRS!*

HOPE I'M NOT *BORIN'* YOU, MAN!

THOP!

CHANCE? HOW'S *THIS* FOR STARTERS?

UH OH! SOMEONE SNEAKING UP *BEHIND* ME!

THE *COSTUMED* ONE FIGHTS LIKE A *MASTER!*

BUT *YOU...* AN UNTUTORED *NOBODY...* SHALL FALL BY MY *IRON FIST!*

MY *DISGUISE!* CAN'T LET HIS *FINGERS* RUB IT OFF!

BUT I CAN DO LOTS *MORE* THAN JUST *DODGE...*

REDWING! GO *GET 'IM!*

SK-RIPP!

HIS *WHIP!* STOP HIM FROM *SNAPPING* IT! *GO,* REDWING!

ACH DU LIEBER! THE BIRD IS NEARLY *HUMAN!*

HE CUT MY *WHIP* WITH HIS *BEAK!*

THIS HAS GONE ON *LONG ENOUGH!* WE WILL *TOY* WITH YOU NO MORE!

MY *MURDER CHAIR* WILL FINISH YOU RIGHT *NOW!*

HEADS UP! HE IS THE DEADLIEST OF *ALL!*

BUT *LOOK!* WE'RE NOT FINISHED *YET!*

19.

THE ONE CALLED THE *FALCON*...HE INSPIRED THE *NATIVES* TO REBEL!

THE *EXILES* CANNOT HOPE TO FIGHT THEM *ALL!*

AND THE ONE *WITH* THE *FALCON*...IT CAN ONLY BE THE *REAL* CAPTAIN AMERICA ...WEARING A CRUDE *DISGUISE!*

HE HAS ESCAPED ME *TOO OFTEN!* THE GAME MUST *END* AT LAST!

IF I DON'T *CRUSH* HIM... HE MAY FIND A WAY TO *FOIL* ME!

AND SO, AVENGER... *YOUR TIME HAS COME... TO DIE!*

ALL OF A SUDDEN..I FEEL STRANGELY *MENACED!*

IT'S THE *CUBE!* THE SKULL IS *WATCHING*...ABOUT TO *STRIKE*...FOR THE *FINAL TIME!*

NEXT **SHOCK** AFTER **SHOCK!**

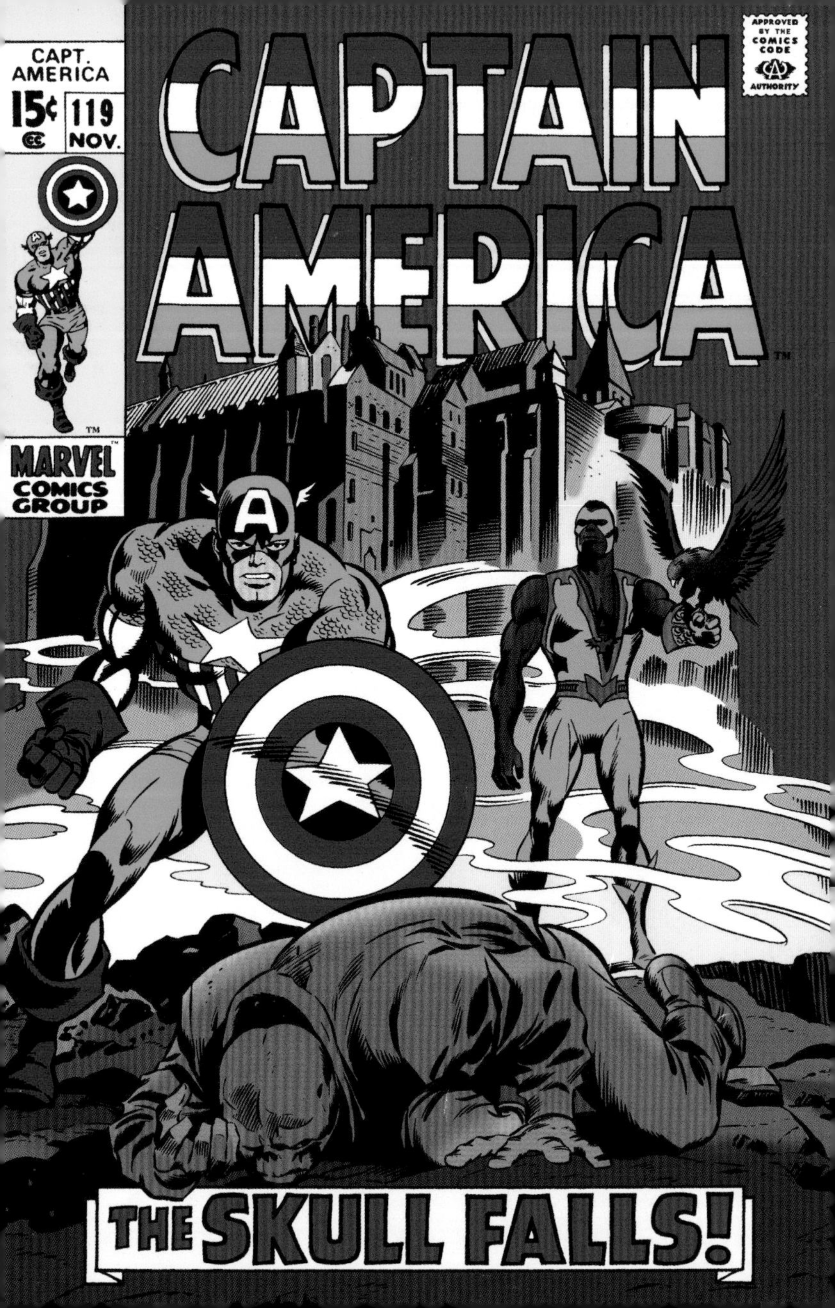
CAPT. AMERICA
15¢
119
NOV.
APPROVED BY THE COMICS CODE AUTHORITY
CAPTAIN AMERICA
MARVEL COMICS GROUP
THE SKULL FALLS!

FIRST, LET ME PUT AN *END* TO THIS MACABRE *MASQUERADE!*

FOR *TOO LONG* HAVE I BEEN HIDDEN IN THE FACE AND FORM OF *CAPTAIN AMERICA!*

IT NO LONGER *AMUSES* ME TO FACE THE WORLD IN SO *DESPICABLE* A ROLE...

...WHEN I CAN *INSTANTANEOUSLY* BE TRANSFORMED INTO THE GLORIOUS, AWESOME IDENTITY WHICH IS MY *BIRTHRIGHT*...

WHEN I CAN BE THE SUPREME *RED SKULL* ONCE MORE!

2.

BUT NOW, *HE* IS *DEAD!* ONLY THE *RED SKULL* STILL REMAINS...TO FULFILL THE NAZI *DREAM!*

SO LONG AS THE *COSMIC CUBE* IS MINE, TYRANNY *YET* SHALL CONQUER THE GLOBE...THE TYRANNY OF THE *RED SKULL!*

BUT FIRST, I MUST *FINISH* THE TASK AT HAND...!

FALCON! DO *YOU* FEEL IT, TOO? THIS STRANGE *SENSATION?*

IT CAN ONLY MEAN *ONE* THING...!

SOMETHING'S *WRONG!* WHAT *IS* IT? *TELL* ME, MAN!

IT'S THE *SKULL!* HE'S *WATCHING*... ABOUT TO *STRIKE!*

HOLD ON! HERE IT COMES...!

4

IT...IT ISN'T *POSSIBLE!* WE MUST...BE *DREAMING!*

IT'S *MY* FAULT, FALCON!

HE'S AFTER *ME!* YOU'RE JUST...AN *INNOCENT BYSTANDER!*

WHEN WE *LAND...* GET *AWAY* FROM ME! *RUN!* THE SKULL MAY LET *YOU* GO!

I'M HIS ENEMY! I'M THE ONE HE'S WAITING TO *DESTROY!*

THE WHOLE THING'S *CRAZY!* BUT WHATEVER HAPPENS....I'M *NOT* RUNNING *OUT!* WE'LL FACE IT *TOGETHER!*

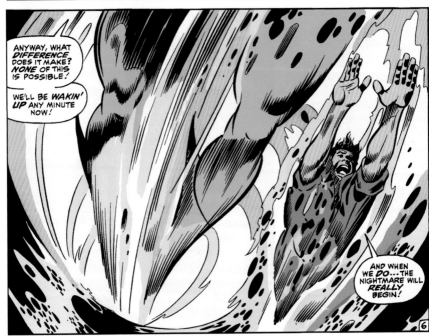

ANYWAY, WHAT *DIFFERENCE* DOES IT MAKE? *NONE* OF THIS IS POSSIBLE!

WE'LL BE *WAKIN'* UP ANY MINUTE NOW!

AND WHEN WE *DO*...THE NIGHTMARE WILL *REALLY* BEGIN!

6

WE'RE HEADING FOR A *CASTLE..!*

THE CASTLE OF...THE *SKULL!*

YOUR MOMENT HAS FINALLY *COME!*

WAIT! DO WHAT YOU WANT TO *ME...* BUT THE *FALCON* HAS NO PART OF THIS!

SILENCE!

I *SAW* YOU BATTLING SIDE-BY-SIDE ON THE *ISLAND OF EXILES!*

ANY ALLY OF *YOURS* IS THE RED SKULL'S SWORN *ENEMY!*

EVEN HIS ACCURSED *BIRD* SHALL SHARE THE *FATE* WHICH MUST BE YOURS!

7.

DID HE THINK I WOULD PERMIT HIM TO *REACH* ME?

YOU'RE A MIGHTY BIG MAN WITH THAT *CUBE* OF YOURS, SKULL!

BUT HOW WOULD YOU BE *WITHOUT* IT?

I'LL *NEVER* BE WITH-OUT IT!

AND NOW, I *TIRE* OF SEE-ING YOU IN THAT PRIMITIVE *DISGUISE!* SO... I WILL *CHANGE* IT!

FOR, WHEN YOU *FALL*... IT MUST BE A SIGHT I WILL ALWAYS *REMEMBER*...

IT MUST BE THE LONG-AWAITED SIGHT OF...

CAPTAIN AMERICA... MEETING HIS FINAL *DEFEAT!*

10

[183]

YOU... THE ONE WHO'S BEEN *HELPING* ME... *TRAINING* ME... WHO MADE ME THE *FALCON*...

YOU'RE CAPTAIN AMERICA!

NEITHER *MY* IDENTITY... NOR *YOURS* HAS ANY *MEANING* NOW! ALL THAT *MATTERS* IS... BEATING THE *SKULL!*

FOOL! IT CANNOT BE *DONE!*

WE'VE GOT TO MAKE HIM *EAT* THOSE WORDS... AND WE *WILL!*

YOU'RE TRYING TO MAKE ME LOSE MY *TEMPER*... TO STRIKE *CARELESSLY* IN HASTE!

WE'VE BATTLED TOO MANY TIMES FOR ME NOT TO KNOW YOUR *TRICKS!*

BUT *THIS* TIME IT WON'T WORK! *THIS* TIME THERE CAN BE BUT *ONE* RESULT...

THIS TIME... YOU DIE!

11.

IN *THAT CASE,* MADMAN... WE'VE GOT NOTHING TO *LOSE!*

BTYONNNG!

A *ROCK!*

I CHARGED AT THE *SKULL* AND SMASHED INTO A *BOULDER!*

NEVER *AGAIN* WILL I FEEL THE STING OF YOUR *SHIELD!*

HE'S... *WITHIN* THE ROCK! PLACED THERE BY... THE *CUBE!*

AND NOW THAT YOU SEE HOW *INVULNERABLE* I AM...

...I HAVE NO *NEED* FOR FURTHER PROTECTION!

HE *SHATTERED* THE ROCK... WITH JUST A *GESTURE!*

HANG *IN* THERE, CAP! THERE'S *GOTTA* BE A WAY TO *TAKE* HIM!

THINK SO, YOU *FOOL...?*

DO YOU SEE HOW *SIMPLE* IT WOULD BE TO *DISPOSE* OF YOU BOTH!

THIS IS THE GREATEST PART OF MY REVENGE... HAVING THE DOOMED *CAPTAIN AMERICA* REALIZE HOW *HELPLESS* HE IS!

THE WATER'S *SUBSIDING!* THERE'S *AIR* AT LAST!

FALCON...ARE YOU OKAY? I THOUGHT YOU'D GONE *UNDER!*

I'M STILL *WITH* IT, CAP...THERE WAS SOMETHING...I HADDA *DO!*

*B*UT, BEFORE WE FIND OUT WHAT THAT SOMETHING *WAS,* AN EVENT IS OCCURRING WITHIN THE HIDDEN HEADQUARTERS OF *AIM* WHICH SOON WILL AFFECT OUR CHARACTERS' LIVES ...

*L*ET US NOW *LISTEN* AS THE MISSHAPEN *MODOK,* SUPER-POWERED OVERLORD OF THE EVIL BROTHERHOOD OF *ADVANCED IDEA MECHANICS,* SPEAKS...

THE COSMIC CUBE IS *OURS!* THE ONE WHO *STOLE* IT MUST NEVER USE IT *AGAINST* US!

WE HEAR THE WORDS OF MIGHTY *MODOK!*

THE CUBE WILL BE *DESTROYED!*

THEN YOU MUST BEGIN *PHASE THREE!*---NOW, WHILE THE WORLD DOES NOT SUS- PECT...

...THAT *MODOK LIVES!*

14

HOW *OFTEN* I EMPLOY MY MYSTIC *MIND SCREEN*... TO RETURN IN MEMORY TO THAT FATEFUL *HOUR!*..

"--WHEN I FOUGHT MY FINAL BATTLE WITH THE SEEMINGLY-TRAPPED *CAPTAIN AMERICA*...*"

*AS PUNGENTLY PORTRAYED IN *TALES OF SUSPENSE* #94, OCT.1967! ...STAN.

"NOT EVEN HIS UBIQUITOUS *SHIELD* COULD PENETRATE MY BLUDGEONING *MENTAL BLAST BEAM*...!"

"BUT, BEFORE I COULD ACHIEVE MY INEVITABLE *VICTORY*, A BAND OF MY OWN DISLOYAL AGENTS *ATTACKED* WITHOUT WARNING..!"

SHOTS... FROM *BEHIND* US! *CAP*... LOOK OUT!

WE'RE NOT THEIR TARGET, SHARON... IT'S *MODOK!*

"AND SO I MET MY FIRST *DEFEAT*

15

"THINKING I WAS *DONE FOR*, THE OTHERS FLED IN MY WAITING *ESCAPE SUB*..."

"...AS MY SHIP WAS *DESTROYED*... WITH *MYSELF* INSIDE!"

"BUT *NONE* COULD SUSPECT THAT I HAD ENCASED MYSELF IN A MENTAL *GLOBE OF FORCE*..."

"...WHICH *SHIELDED* ME FROM THE IMPACT ...AND PROVIDED *AIR* TO BREATHE!"

"IT WAS A *SIMPLE* MATTER TO EMIT A MENTAL *SONIC BEAM* TO WHERE MY OTHER AGENTS WOULD RECEIVE IT..."

"AND SO I WAS *FOUND*, BROUGHT *BACK*, AND RESTORED TO *LEADERSHIP* ONCE MORE!"

NOW, ALL THAT REMAINS IS TO *ACTIVATE* OUR POTENT *CATHOLITE BLOCK* ...WHICH SHALL *END* THE POWER OF THE *COSMIC CUBE!*

BETTER TO *DESTROY* OUR GREATEST CREATION, THAN ALLOW IT TO SERVE *ANOTHER'S* WILL!

AND SO WE SHALL BEGIN... *PHASE THREE!*

16.

MEANWHILE, WHAT OF *CAP* AND THE *FALCON?* THIS IS A PERFECT TIME TO FIND *OUT*...

THE *WATER*... IT'S CHANGING INTO *SAND!*

THE *SKULL'S* LIKE AN EXCITED *KID* WITH SOME WONDROUS NEW *TOY*... HE CAN'T GET *ENOUGH* OF IT!

WE'RE DRIFTING *UPWARD*... INTO THE *AIR!*

SECONDS LATER... OR IS IT *MINUTES*... OR *HOURS?* SO WEAK AND DEPLETED ARE CAP AND THE FALCON THAT THEY SEEM TO LOSE ALL SENSE OF TIME... OF SPACE... OF *ANYTHING*... SAVE THEIR OWN GNAWING, NAGGING, ACHING, ALMOST UNENDURABLE *FATIGUE!* AND THEN AT LAST...

WE'VE *LANDED*... BUT *WHERE?*

WHAT DOES IT *MATTER?* ...AS LONG AS... WE CAN *REST*... FOR A FEW MINUTES!

THERE HE *IS*... STANDING... *WATCHING* US! IT LOOKS LIKE... OUR TIME HAS *COME!*

BUT... WE WON'T GIVE UP! IF... YOU CAN MANAGE... TO *DISTRACT* HIM...

IT SEEMS *HOPELESS*... BUT, IF CAP SAYS *DO* IT...

A FINAL *CHARGE*, EH? YOU'LL NEVER COMPLETE IT... *ALIVE!*

17.

OH **NO** YOU DON'T!

THE **FALCON!**

CAP'S ALMOST **DONE IN**...AND I'M NOT MUCH **BETTER!**

BUT I'VE **GOT** TO DELAY HIM... GOT TO **STOP** HIM... SOMEHOW!

I **DID** IT! BUT... HE'S STILL **FRESH**...AT THE PEAK OF HIS **STRENGTH**...

WHILE **I**... HOW MUCH LONGER...CAN I HOLD **ON**?

WHAT ARE THEY **MADE** OF? EVEN ON THE VERGE OF **EXHAUSTION**... THEY KEEP FIGHTING **ON!**

BUT THE CUBE IS STILL **MINE!** I CAN **WILL** IT...TO COME CLOSER ...AND **CLOSER** TO ME...UNTIL...!

I **HAVE** IT AGAIN!

BUT **WAIT!** WHAT'S **HAPPENING** TO IT? IT...IT'S **CHANGING**... GROWING **FORMLESS**... BEGINNING TO **MELT!**

NOW, REDWING... **NOW!** ATTACK! **ATTACK!**

NO! NO!

19